Percy

Hathaway House, Book 16

Dale Mayer

PERCY: HATHAWAY HOUSE, BOOK 16
Beverly Dale Mayer
Valley Publishing Ltd.

ISBN-13: 978-1-773365-78-7
Print Edition

Books in This Series

About This Book

Welcome to Hathaway House. Rehab Center. Safe Haven. Second chance at life and love.

It was Aaron who convinced Percy to take a chance on Hathaway House. Yet, when he arrives, Aaron is back at school, and Percy's alone after all. The place is everything Aaron said it was, but the trip getting here set his progress back, from slow to nonexistent.

Giada has worked at the center for several years and always went home happily to her brother at the end of the day. Only now her brother is engaged and planning to marry in six months. Change is happening, whether she likes it or not. And, in this case, it brings up a lot of turbulence in the family dynamic. Dani offers Giada a place of her own here at Hathaway's staff quarters, but the path forward is not so easy. Thankfully Percy is there as both a comfort and a friend.

Now if only he could find the progress he's looking for, and she could find the new beginning of her own …

Sign up to be notified of all Dale's releases here!

https://geni.us/DaleNews

Prologue

P ERCY ERWIN STARED down at the application. It had come in the mail from his old friend Aaron. He read the letter that went with it, looked at the application, and shook his head. He immediately picked up his phone and sent a text to Aaron. **Got your application.**

Good, fill it out.

Are you sure, man?

Get your butt to Hathaway House, he texted. **With any luck, I'll be there too.**

You still healing?

No, read the letter. I'm almost a vet by now.

Animal vet? At that, his phone rang.

"I'm almost done with school to become a veterinarian," he said. "And I'm marrying the owner of Hathaway. But you need to be here because here's where the magic happens."

"I'm not sure I'm up for it, man. That last surgery was three months ago, and I'm still not back on my feet."

"Which is why you need to be here," he argued. "Besides, you're missing a foot. How can you be on both feet if you're missing one?"

"*Ha, ha,*" Percy said. "The leg's all messed up."

"So, if you don't have a leg, you don't have a leg. If you got a bum leg, you got a bum leg. Come here and start dealing with it."

"What makes Hathaway so special?"

"You know what? I've been trying to explain that to a lot of people for a long time," he said. "I don't really have anything as an answer. Except for incredible results. What I can tell you is, it is special. I guarantee it."

"*Hmm*," he said.

"Just deal with it, get that application in, and come."

"If it's that good, I'm sure there's a heck of a waiting list."

"There is," he said. "But I put your name down when I heard you went back in for surgery again."

"You what?"

"Yep," he said. "I know you weren't ready three months ago, and you still had a lot of work to do, but you're only as healed as much as you feel it."

"And that isn't very much."

"Which is why you need to come here," he said. "I can't force you. So, fill it out and send it in. Or better yet, just fill it out, take a photo of it, and send it to me."

"It'll hardly be that fast," he said.

"No, there's all kinds of other paperwork to be done."

"I don't do paperwork."

"Stop being difficult," Aaron said. "I mean it, man. I carried your sorry butt through the jungle to save you one time, and I'll do it again, if I have to."

"This is hardly to save me."

"And that's where you're wrong. This *is* to save you. You have no idea what a different person you'll be after a few months here."

"Are you serious?"

"Never more serious in my life," he replied. "Please, if you can't do this for you, do it for me."

"Man, I don't think I'm ready for more of this."

"Like I said, you don't know what you've got, and you don't know what you're capable of, until you're here."

He sighed and said, "Okay, but I'm only going to fill this out, take a photo of it, and then I'll come whenever it's approved."

"Good," he said. "I'll do the rest."

"Not likely," he said. "There'll be all kinds of things to deal with for this to go through."

"But it's worth it," Aaron said cheerfully on the other side.

"I'm only doing this because you say so."

"I saved your life back then," Aaron said, "and, honest to goodness, this will save your life too."

Chapter 1

P ERCY ERWIN WAS already in bed in his assigned room at Hathaway House and glared at the email on his phone. "Why are you not here, Aaron?" he snapped to no one in particular. When a cough came at the open door to his room, he lifted his gaze to a young woman, a bright, cheerful smile on her face and a clipboard in her hand. He groaned. "Sorry, I shouldn't be showing my impatience," he muttered.

She stepped forward, gave him a gentle smile. "I'm Dani, and Aaron was really hoping you would get in last week before he had to leave for school. But we had a mix-up on the beds and had to postpone your arrival."

"And"—he lifted his stump—"I had an infection that held me back anyway."

She nodded. "Aaron will be back for a long weekend here soon. Next month I think."

Percy settled back into bed and studied her. He'd heard so much from Aaron over the last few months about *his Dani*, but, at the same time, it didn't do her justice. "You're really marrying him, huh?"

A beautiful smile beamed once again from her face, and she nodded cheerfully. "I sure hope so. We just have to get through a little bit more first. We've got plans happening all the time."

"This year?"

"I think next spring," she replied. "He's in an accelerated program, and, with any luck, he should be done come April."

Percy's eyebrows shot up at that. "Hard to imagine the guy I used to know as a veterinarian."

"In a way," she murmured, "he always was a vet. It was his first love."

"And again that seems hard to believe too. I knew him in the navy," he murmured. "And he was definitely not the same person."

"No, he went in because of his brother," she noted.

"I remember hearing something about him. Levi, I think."

"Yes, Levi," she confirmed.

And didn't her dimples peek out when she tilted her lips in a certain way. He was fascinated and, at the same time, envious of everything that Aaron had found. "A wife and a new career and apparently, according to him, a whole new view of life and health."

At that, she chuckled. "He was one of our first success stories," she admitted, "but I'm grateful to say that we have hundreds of them now."

"Well, I'm hoping I can be another one." Percy shifted in bed.

She studied him. "It's not just the leg, is it?"

He shook his head. "A piece of shrapnel is in my spine that they can't remove for danger of paralyzing me."

She winced at that. "I'm sorry. That's a tough one. Have you gotten a second opinion on that?"

"No, I haven't bothered." He reached out an arm to snag the water, but, as sometimes happened, he overreached and, instead of grabbing it, knocked it over.

She immediately walked forward and picked it up. "And that's one of the reasons why we keep lids on them," she noted cheerfully, as she handed it to him.

He took it and had a long sip of water, before relaxing again.

"You're having some arm coordination problems too?"

He nodded. "It's all in the folder." He closed his eyes, took in a long heavy breath, and let it out very slowly, as in tiny increments.

"And back pain," she added, with a nod.

He opened his eyes, studied her. "Why don't we just say that all of me is a mess? Top to bottom."

"The good news is," she replied, "we specialize in that."

He searched her face to see if she were serious, but she appeared to be. "Aaron told me a miracle is here for me."

"Miracles require help though," she pointed out in a sweet voice. "That is something for you to remember."

"Meaning?"

"We can offer the miracle, but it's up to you to reach for it and to make it your own." And, with that, she gave him the gentlest of smiles. "I'll see you later. Press the Call button on your bed if you need anything." And she stepped out of his room.

But she left him with something to think about—something he hadn't really considered. Yet she was right. If he wanted a miracle here, he would have to reach with both hands to accept what was offered and would have to do the work required. Too bad Aaron hadn't warned Percy about that. With a shake of his head, he snatched his phone and sent Aaron a quick text message, saying he had just met Dani. **She has a definite way about her ...**

Not expecting an answer, he put his phone back down and reached again for the cup, this time a little more carefully, knowing that, if he were the one who had to get out of bed to pick it up off the floor, he would regret it. In fact, it would stay on the floor, as that effort was just more than he could handle. He had finished the water and had set aside the empty cup, when a tap came at the door. He looked up to see a tall and very fit male standing in the open doorway, smiling at him. "Hey. Who are you?"

"Shane," he murmured. "I'm on your team. Has Dani been through here yet?"

"She was just here."

"Good. As long as she's introduced herself, I'll go over the formalities." He picked up the folder that Dani had left. "And I'll explain the Hathaway House system to you."

By the time Shane finished talking, Percy could almost feel his head trying to explode. "So the gist of it is, everybody assigned to me will come to me to introduce themselves. Then I'll follow the schedules in my tablet, when I have the time and energy to look at it."

"That's just about it," Shane replied in a cheerful voice.

"Is everybody here so cheerful?" Percy groused.

Shane laughed, shaking his head. "Nope, not always. You'll find a lot of the other patients know exactly how much it takes to make them cry," he noted quietly. "As far as the staff, we try to be compassionate, caring, and upbeat."

"The upbeat part gets a bit much."

"Then you'll be happy to see it some days because everything else in your world may look like storm clouds otherwise."

"Sometimes it's nice to know that the sun's on the other side," he muttered, staring at the tall, very fit man that Percy already didn't want to be around because Shane was just a reminder of who and what Percy used to be. "Yet we don't want it to break through because that means we have to face it."

Shane stopped and looked at him quietly for a long moment. "Interesting philosophy. You can also turn that around and see that the rays of sunshine mean that you *can* break through the cloud to the other side." He looked at Percy, handed him the folder, gave him the iPad, and turned it on for him. "I'll leave you to go over your schedule. Sounds like we'll have a lot of fun here."

"What in any of that means *fun?*" he asked.

At the doorway Shane stopped, turned, and looked at him. "You might need a little attitude adjustment, but I have no doubt that you'll get that soon enough."

"And what would bring *that* on?" he murmured. "I used to be like you," he admitted. "Fit, strong, could bench press incredible weights. Gymnastics, sports, whatever. It didn't matter. I was up for it. From heavy physical sports to martial arts."

"Good to know," Shane stated. "I guess that's what the goal is then, isn't it? Which one of those really matters the most?"

"What do you mean?"

"Well, does sports matter most to you? Or do the martial arts matter more? Does it matter to return to snowboarding or skiing? Do you want to paddleboard? What is *the one thing* that you really miss the most and that you would really strive for?"

"I don't think there is just one," he murmured, staring at Shane in puzzlement. "Why? You can't give it to me."

"Absolutely I can give it to you," Shane argued, his voice

calm, patient. "It just depends on how much you really want it."

And, with that, just like Dani, Shane left with that heavy-weighted shot that gave Percy so much more to think about. As he wondered about that, he had to question if it were really possible. He stared down at his phone. Even though Aaron had yet to answer Percy's last text, he quickly texted his friend again. **Is weight-lifting even possible again?**

When the response came back, Aaron texted **Yes. You might be surprised. Find the one thing that you really care about. That, if you could return to it, you would feel recovered. Get it clear in your mind and use that as a goal post. When you reach it, we'll both celebrate.**

Percy stared at his phone, as he slowly laid it on the bedside beside him. "Jesus."

To even think that something like that could be possible again was almost too much for him to believe. As far as he was concerned, these were all pipe dreams.

His previous doctors had told him that he'd never walk normally again. Other doctors told him that he would never sit for a long period because of the shrapnel. Still another one stated that disability benefits were for people like him. Like how was any of that geared to make Percy feel like a man again? A whole, healthy contributing-to-society and functioning man? Where in all that doom and gloom did Hathaway House find any hope for Percy? So what was so different about this place?

Yet he'd already seen something was different. Yet his tight ball of anger remained in his throat, locking down his chest, tightly locking in the words that he wanted to get out. But, for the first time, he had to wonder if he hadn't tripped into a wonderland of some kind. As if the people here were talking in a language that he didn't recognize, as if they saw something in him that he didn't see in himself.

None of it made any sense. And yet, for the first time—and maybe because none of it made sense—he could see that he was somewhere completely foreign. Maybe because it wasn't exactly what he'd been through over and over again, maybe this time the end result could be different.

GIADA TIASCO PUSHED the cart down the hallway, watching as Shane left the room that she was heading to, with a supply of new towels, just delivered this morning. At the open doorway she knocked, stuck her head around, and asked, "Do you mind yet another interruption?" The patient looked at her, and she noted not anger so much but a sense of *loss* maybe.

"I have fresh towels and a couple spare blankets for you," she stated, ignoring the look in his eyes. She quickly brought in the towels, stocked up the bathroom, and placed one of his blankets over the end of the bed. She noted the missing foot and completely ignored it. She'd seen so much worse in this place. With the second blanket, she walked over to the closet and stored it there. "In case you don't know, your personal belongings are in here, and I'll put this extra blanket for you here too."

"Thank you."

She nodded and stepped towards the door.

"I mean it, thank you."

"Not a problem." She tossed him a gentle smile. "It looks like you aren't having a good day."

"I just arrived," he muttered.

"Ouch. Those are the worst days."

He looked at her with interest. "You mean, there are bad days?" he teased. "It seems like everybody here is living on sunshine and roses."

She chuckled. "Not always. This isn't my normal job, but I'm doing this today. We're short-staffed right now because, you know, somebody's day wasn't sunshine and roses. But that doesn't matter because we all pitch in to help."

"You don't mind running laundry carts around the place?" he asked doubtfully. "Unless of course your other job would be to grab cleaning cloths."

She crossed her arms, leaned against the open doorway, but she smiled. "I guess to you it probably seems that way, doesn't it?"

"I would do a lot to avoid scrubbing anything," he admitted.

"And sometimes it's just nice to do something that's menial. It's mindless, and you don't have to focus on it because you already know how to do it, like riding a bike, so it's no pressure, no extra stress in your day."

"Agreed," he stated. "Just never been anything that I've really needed to do."

"You might find something you like that's good for you. That's why some people do puzzles or crosswords or just something mindless to take them away from the scenario that they're dealing with daily."

"Maybe." Percy shrugged. "I can't say I've ever found anything like that which works for me."

"Or that you haven't tried to find something yet because you haven't needed to," she noted shrewdly. He looked uncomfortable, even as he lay in the bed, as if stiff and sore. "You are obviously in a lot of pain. Do you want me to get you a nurse?"

He looked up at her and asked, "How can you tell I'm in pain?"

"Just the way you're positioned in bed."

"You're the second person to comment on how uncomfortable I look. It seems normal to me."

"It's normal because you're out of tune with your body," she noted. He glared at her. "Sorry." She held up a hand. "And I'm known for being blunt."

"Generally I don't mind blunt," he muttered. "But it's a little rough when everybody here seems to know something about me that I don't even recognize."

"And again," she stated, as she walked toward him, "everything inside you is out of alignment. I've been here long enough to know."

"And are you like a physio or a doctor or something, when you're not pushing laundry carts around?"

Chapter 2

"**N**OPE, I'M THE purchaser for the place," Giada replied, chuckling. "Dani's job got too big, and she had to split off a bunch of her job duties to other people."

"A purchaser?"

She smiled, as she leaned against the small table at his bedside. "Yes. I'm responsible for keeping stock of everything on the property, of everything in the place. And watching the budgets."

"Interesting," he murmured. "So it's a business-type job."

"Yes, and again that's not a negative in my world."

"No, it doesn't have to be," he replied. "I don't even know what I'm thinking anymore. I'm sure this place needs a lot of supplies."

"You have no idea." She laughed again. "It's huge. And getting bigger all the time."

"Well, I'm here now," he noted, "so I'll add to the usage of toilet paper and soap."

"And, if you need anything special," she murmured, "tell me."

"*Special?*"

"Absolutely. Something that would make this place easier or a little bit more like home for you. You only have to let me know."

"That's not normal," he stated.

"No, it's not, but we don't run Hathaway House like it's normal," she murmured. "Same as with the food." At that, his stomach growled. She smiled. "Have you made it down there yet?"

"No." Percy shook his head. "I won't be making it anywhere today."

"How about I get you a tray?"

He frowned. "No, I think doing laundry duty is enough. You don't have to be the waitress too."

"Hey, you," she said, pointing at him, while smiling, "you don't know enough about how this place works yet to make that kind of a decision. Honest to God, we all do whatever we need to do to make it work."

"I can't ask you to get me a tray," he protested.

"And why not?" she asked, giving him a flat stare. She watched as the color rose up his neck. "Or I can wheelchair you there, and you can pick out something for yourself." She watched the immediate negative reaction on his face. "Got it. In that case, I'll go find you some food. Do you want a hot cup of coffee?" When she mentioned coffee, she saw the want in his eyes. She nodded. "Okay, so coffee it is. How do you take it?"

"Black," he replied instantly. "And I really, really would appreciate a cup of coffee."

"Oh, that's a done deal for me too," she murmured. "I start my day with that every morning. I'd be lifeless without it."

He smiled. "Well, that's nice to know that we have something in common," he mentioned, with a gentle chuckle. "Now if only ... Do they have other food there too?"

She understood what he meant. "Yes. Are you on a special diet?"

"No, except I'm always hungry these days."

"That's a good sign," she noted. "It means your body's healing."

He frowned at her again.

"That's all right. They'll figure it out here, and they'll get you on the straight and narrow again. Now when it comes to food …" She looked at her watch. "It's two-thirty. How about something like a cinnamon bun, or do you need real food? Like a bowl of soup and a sandwich?"

He studied her to see if she were serious and then shrugged. "Something a little more solid would help. I didn't eat any breakfast because I was traveling this morning."

"And you came by ambulance?"

He nodded. "I gather that's the most popular way."

"Well, it's the best way," she noted. "I'll leave my cart here and go see what Dennis has on offer."

"Dennis?"

She laughed. "Dennis runs the front of the kitchen. Whatever you want, he'll get you."

"Well, if you see Dennis, and he's got any food, I'd appreciate it."

And, with that, she turned and walked back out again and headed toward the dining room. As she pushed open the doors to the dining area, Dennis was vacuuming. He saw her, shut down the vacuum, pulled out his earplugs, and she heard Beyoncé coming through, loud and clear. She smiled at him. "Listening to anybody as high energy as her, I wonder that you aren't dancing while you do this."

He chuckled. "Well, if you hadn't come in, I probably would be dancing any moment. What can I do for you?"

"Anything for a new arrival? He didn't have breakfast, hasn't had lunch, and he was hoping for some *real food.* However, I think light is the way to go. I suggested soup and a sandwich, but I'm not sure if that's even doable. However, he definitely wants a black coffee."

Dennis frowned, as he walked to the back. "I've got a few things here that might work for him. I knew we had a couple people coming in today, but I hadn't heard that they had arrived."

"He's in room 314," she noted. "I think he's a friend of Aaron's."

"I think you're right. Not that that'll make any difference around here, but I do know that Aaron said to treat him right."

"Of course we'll treat him right," she replied. "We treat them all right. The question is whether we have anything to offer him right now or whether he needs to wait a little bit."

At that, he stared at her in shock. "Wait? For food? I mean, you did come to me, right?" She laughed again. "I'll take it to him, if you're busy," Dennis offered.

"He probably should meet you anyway, but he's too tired and beat for a trip to the dining room."

"In that case, I'll come back with you, introduce myself, and we'll see what he wants for dinner."

"Well, right now, I'm pretty sure he could use something to hold him over."

He agreed. "I've got a nice beef and barley soup back here. Let me get him a bowl to take with us. What about food allergies?" he asked over his shoulder, as he headed into the kitchen.

"Not any that he mentioned."

When Dennis returned, he had a large bowl and off to

the side was a big thick ham and cheese sandwich. It looked like every vegetable under the sun had been tucked between the two slices of bread. She stared at the sandwich in awe. "How come things like that aren't on offer when I come in for lunch?"

"They are," he replied. "You just have to ask."

She shook her head. "I would never ask you for special dishes. You're always so busy as it is. I won't add to your workload. I work here too. I'm not even a patient."

He gave her a hard glance and wagged a finger at her. "And I don't ever want to hear you say that again because, without the staff, we are nothing."

"Got it," she admitted, with half a sigh. "And I do get that. I just feel bad taking food that's supposed to be for the patients."

"There's enough food for everybody, the staff included. You know that's how it works."

"I ... know," she hesitantly agreed.

"It's because of your particular job," he noted, shaking his head. "You know what the bills look like, so you're always trying to keep your portion down."

"You know what? You could be right," she admitted. "Just like the rest of us, we're invested in this place, and we want to make sure it runs for a very long time."

"You're not kidding," he declared. "Now"—and he picked up the tray—"lead the way."

She led him back down to where the patient was. "I don't even know his name," she admitted. "I was delivering towels and blankets and spoke to him a bit."

Dennis looked at her, laughed, and asked, "What are you doing delivering towels and blankets?"

"Two of the housekeeping staff called in sick today," she

replied.

At that, Dennis rolled his eyes. "Yep, that explains it. A couple illnesses around town have hit people pretty hard. I know we're not the only place that's been hit."

They were already at the door. She tapped it gently, stuck her head around the open door again, and announced, "Food delivery." She stepped inside.

Dennis followed, and he walked closer to the small bedside table, placed his tray there, and shifted it closer to where the patient was.

Giada stepped forward. "This is Dennis. He's the one who runs the kitchen. If there's anything you want, you just tell him." Then she looked down at the patient, the man who even now stared up at the huge man at her side in surprise. "I didn't catch your name when I was first here."

He looked at her now and replied, "I'm Percy."

"Good. I'm Giada, and, like I said, this is Dennis." Then she studied the position of Percy's bed. "You can't eat like that though. I can either help you reposition the bed or do you have the remote?" She looked around for it and saw it on the window ledge. She walked over, grabbed it. "Here. You can adjust the bed as you need to." He grabbed the remote with relief and pushed some buttons to shift the angle of his bed. She watched as some of Percy's pain eased back. "I'm sorry. I should have mentioned this earlier."

He looked at her in surprise. "Why? I am mobile," he noted. "I have crutches and a wheelchair. I could have got it myself."

"You could have," she agreed cheerfully, "but I think, after today's travels, even just lying in bed is enough effort for anybody." And, with that, she stepped back. "Dennis also wants to know what you might want for dinner. So you guys can chat about that, while I head back to the office." She smiled at Dennis. "Thanks for bringing in the food." She gave them both a three-finger wave and left.

PERCY STARED UP at Dennis. "Now that she's gone, could I ask a favor?"

Dennis looked at him immediately and asked, "What's up?"

"I need a little help shifting over to the left," he admitted. "I've kind of gone numb."

Immediately Dennis walked over to the left, and, gently using his hands, slid them under Percy's knees and behind his shoulders and slowly shifted him over a few inches.

As soon as Dennis did that, Percy whispered, "Thank God for that. The pain was killing me."

"Do you get the paralysis much?"

"Too much," Percy admitted. "It's nerve damage, kicks in and off again. Sometimes it's not bad, but the trip today was a little more than I had bargained for."

"It often is," Dennis agreed. "One of the hardest responsibilities we have is getting people to understand that this journey can set you back. It can set you back a little bit, or it can set you back a lot. And we don't do anything harsh for the first few days. We don't, in fact, do *anything* for those first few days in most cases," he noted, with a smile, "because of the trip."

"That's good to know," he shared. "I was a little worried that I'd have to get up and show what I can and cannot do tomorrow."

"Nope, you do what you can do, and you tell them

when you can't do something," Dennis stated calmly. "They'll know if you're lying or if you haven't been pushing yourself enough. They're really good at seeing that," he noted. "But, when you're still injured, and you're not handling the trip very well, do not overtax yourself, or it'll send you right back to the VA hospital. And we don't want that, if we can avoid it. So I've got food for you now," he noted, "and I hope that this selection is okay. I brought you a beef and barley soup and a big sandwich. And, if you tell me what you'd like for dinner, I'll make sure I get a tray down to you. I can't guarantee it'll be delivered by me, but I'll make sure I get one to you."

"And that would be awesome if you could. I don't know what kind of food I can even ask for."

"Is there anything you like?"

"Everything," he stated. "I'm always empty these days."

Dennis looked at him in surprise. "That's better than what we often get told. So many times we get guys here who have lost their appetite and can't eat or too many body functions were difficult, so they were refusing to eat, or sometimes the pain meds they were on affected their appetite. So, if you've got an appetite, we'll feed it," he stated. "Are you up for beef, chicken, fish?"

"All of the above," he murmured. "And I sure could go with like a baked potato or some mashed potatoes, gravy, vegetables. I really do like my vegetables. But I especially crave protein right now."

"And you need the protein for muscle building," he noted instantly. "I didn't bring the coffee though." He frowned at that. "I think she promised you a coffee."

"She did, but I guess it got forgotten," he said. "That's all right. I can wait."

"Nope. You tuck into the food. I'll go grab the coffee and return. I'm just cleaning up in the dining area anyway." And, with that, Dennis booked it from the room. Percy stared at the tray, managed to push it a little bit closer, lowered the bed level a bit, so the food was easier to reach, and he stared at the sandwich in awe. "The fact that it's even holding together is amazing."

He picked up a spoon, with not very high expectations. He took a sip of the soup and froze. Then another sip and another. "Dear God," he whispered, "it's food. Like it's *really* food."

Female laughter lifted toward him.

He looked up to see an older woman in the doorway, smiling at him. "That's one of the best surprises when you come here." She waved at him. "Keep eating. Nothing like having a hot meal, especially when you're hungry." He nodded and kept an eye on her but proceeded to keep eating the soup. "I'm one of the doctors on your team, and I'll see you on a regular basis."

"Doctor of?"

"Psychiatry," she replied gently. He winced. She nodded and smiled. "And that is a response I'm quite accustomed to getting. Not to worry. We'll get to the problems that you have to deal with in due time."

"What makes you think I have any?" he asked, challenging her.

"Well, you're here. You're recovering from something traumatic," she explained. "Therefore, you have something to deal with."

"Is it that simple?"

"Absolutely. Figuring out what other issues you're dealing with? Not so much." She shrugged. "However, we will get there, and we'll do it in your time, in your space, so that you don't get stressed over it all."

"Is that even possible?" he asked, studying her carefully. She had salt-and-pepper hair, a buxom frame, but her no-nonsense direct approach was very appealing.

"Absolutely," she declared. "Now finish your meal because the food here is delicious, and we want to make sure you get as much as you need to eat. Dinner is supposed to be a Spanish theme tonight, I think. I heard talk of paella." She smiled. "And I absolutely love paella." And, with that, she was gone.

<h1 style="text-align:center">Chapter 3</h1>

G IADA HEADED BACK to her office. She had her own close to Dani's.

As she walked past, Dani looked up and said, "We have a new patient."

Giada nodded. "I just met him." She stepped into Dani's office. "He looks a little overwhelmed. He's a friend of Aaron's. And I know we get new patients on an almost daily basis, but I know that this guy's important to Aaron. Not as if we didn't get a heads-up that he was coming," she added, with a tinkling laugh.

Dani winced. "I made it a little bit heavy, didn't I?"

"That's all right. You know that nobody will suffer, and we're all aware that he needs help."

"Yeah, I probably shouldn't even have mentioned it, so he gets treated the same as everybody else."

"It's all good," Giada said, with a wave. "Dennis is getting him food right now."

"Oh, good." Dani checked the wall clock.

"He needed something, and I promised him coffee and then completely forgot, when I got into the kitchen. Dennis was helpful enough to make up something and to take it to Percy's room, and then I disappeared and forgot the coffee." She gave an eye roll. "Well, it gives an excuse for one of us to go check on him again. I think I'll leave that in Dennis's capable hands. I was delivering towels and blankets."

Dani looked up in surprise.

Giada shrugged. "I know we're short-handed today. I was down there counting inventory, and Simone was looking for somebody to give her a hand, so I just spent a half hour with Percy."

"You have a good heart," Dani noted quietly.

"Everybody who's here does," she added. "I'm nobody different, nobody special."

At that, Dani burst out laughing. "Man, if only we saw ourselves as others see us. I see a woman who saw a need and who filled it without question. You spoke to a new patient, made him feel better, arranged to get him food, besides your job to ensure we get all the supplies here into the center that we need."

"It helps me a lot if I walk around and see what people do need."

Dani chuckled. "Whatever helps you and the others is fine by me. Also I have an apartment here, available soon, if you want to move onto the campus."

"Nope, that's okay," she replied. "I'm okay in town. Besides, it's just ten minutes out."

"I know." Dani looked a little troubled. "But you realize that so many other employees get that perk. And I can't compensate you for not getting housing here."

At that, Giada laughed. "You'd break my brother's heart if you persuaded me to move here."

"Right, but he's getting married soon."

"Not for at least six months," she said cheerfully. "So I have six months to figure it out."

"Just say the word, and I promise that we'll have a place for you in six months."

At that, she nodded. "You'll only have a place if some-body quits, moves, or if you build another building."

"Believe me. I do think about adding more living spac-es," she stated, with a heavy sigh. "But I've got so much else going on right now."

"And you've just done an expansion, getting in more beds and all the equipment."

"I know. If we didn't have all the grant money, we would be really hobbled."

"Don't you worry about it," Giada noted. "I'm working on keeping us on a budget."

"Wouldn't that be nice," Dani muttered, as she went back to her paperwork.

Giada headed back to her office, sat down, and buried herself in her work. About an hour later she lifted her head and realized that she herself had skipped out on lunch and hadn't even gotten coffee. Frowning at that, she checked her watch and noted she still had an hour to go before dinner was served. She headed to the dining room and poured herself a coffee. Dennis caught sight of her, with a hail. "Hey." She smiled at him. "Thanks for the help earlier."

He shook his head. "*De nada*. Everybody deserves help in this place." He looked at her coffee. "I don't remember seeing you at lunch today." He frowned.

"How can you possibly have a photographic memory and keep tabs on all of us?"

"Because I like to see everything running perfectly, and that means you guys all need to be fed," he scolded.

"I'm staying late and working," she shared, "so maybe I'll have dinner here."

"Definitely have dinner here. You know your meals are covered anyway."

"I know, but my brother is back at home," she mentioned, "so I like to go home for him too."

Dennis nodded wisely. "Family's important. Besides, isn't that brother of yours getting married?"

She burst out laughing. "You and Dani are busy keeping tabs on even my family, but you're right, he is."

"So you should move here," he said instantly.

She rolled her eyes. "And again you sound like a Dani parrot." He almost looked offended at that comment. And then she rushed forward to say, "Meaning that you're both very caring." He looked somewhat mollified by that. He looked down at her coffee again and asked, "Are you sure you don't want something to eat with that?"

"I don't want anything sweet," she replied. "It will ruin dinner."

"How about some cheese and crackers or some fruit and cheese?" At that, her spirits lifted, and her stomach growled on cue. "Give me a minute." Dennis disappeared into the back.

She stood here waiting, looking around at the massive space and the outdoor patio. A meeting was going on in one corner inside; several people were outside seated at the tables. When Dennis showed up again, Giada's eyebrows shot up, and her smile beamed. "Now that's gorgeous. Berries, grapes, and watermelon."

"Yep. Here's a few crackers and cheese to go with it. That's just to keep the nibblies down, while you work."

She snorted at that. "If I let you feed me all the time, I'll gain twenty-five pounds."

"Ha! You could use it." Then he waved at her. "Go on, back to work with you."

"Do you think Percy will make it down for dinner?" she

asked, after she got a few steps away, turning back and frowning at Dennis. "I got the impression that he was trying for the tough guy act but wasn't doing very well."

"I know, but day one's brutal."

"I heard day two's worse."

He laughed. "It can be, and it can take them three or four days before they're ready to get started with their rehab routine."

"It seems so sad that just the trip here should take the stuffing right out of them."

"They've got a lot of things to adjust to," he noted quietly. "Don't you worry. I'll go back and ensure he's got dinner." Then he stopped and added, "Unless you want to take it to him."

"Naw, probably better that you do."

"Nope," he stated firmly, "much better for a guy like that to have a beautiful woman bring him a meal. Believe me. He'll eat more if you take it than if I do."

She shook her head. "That's baloney."

"Prove it to me," he dared her.

"Nope," she said, as she headed to the double doors. "If I'm still around, you can always tag me." And she escaped back to her office. Her tray was full, and, when she walked past Shane, he took one look at the fruit and cheese platter, and he almost crowed.

"Oh, my," he said, "I keep forgetting that we can ask Dennis for specialties like that."

"I didn't even ask," she cried out in protest. "He just wouldn't let me have straight caffeine."

"That's probably a good thing. Did he grill you as to whether you'd eaten yet today?"

"Did he ever, and, of course, he didn't see me at

lunchtime 'cause I worked through lunch," she admitted, with a heavy sigh. "So this is in lieu of."

"And you're staying for that meeting tonight, aren't you?"

She nodded. "So I told him that I'd show up for dinner."

Shane laughed. "And he probably already knows exactly what your favorite dish is, and you can expect it for dinner."

"Well, I don't even know that I have a favorite dish," she shared, "so that's pretty easy." And she kept on walking.

By the time she lifted her head for the meeting, she was already running behind. She grabbed her pen and paper and her iPad and raced into the boardroom. Twelve of them were participating right now. And the meeting was intense, regarding lots of budgetary issues, and she was one of the ones intent to send items to the chopping block so that they stayed within the proposed numbers. By the time she was done with her portion of the meeting, she sagged beside Dani in relief.

Dani reached over, patted Giada's hand, and said, "You did really well."

And the only reason Giada did so well was because she was trying to keep things in check. But some of the supplies needed to be pulled back a bit. How did one do that when cleanliness was paramount? And of course the grocery budget? She would not be the one to tell Dennis or Ilse that they needed to cut back in the kitchen. They'd already done that several times in the last couple years, and they were doing really well to stay as top-notch as they did now.

By the time the meeting was over, and the rest of the staff members got up and left, Dani looked at Giada. "Come on. Let's go have dinner."

"What? Did you get the memo that I was staying too?" She laughed.

"Dennis told me."

"That man." Giada shook her head. "He's so busy looking after us all that surely he needs somebody to look after him."

"He so does," Dani agreed. "I keep hoping he'll find a perfect partner."

"For that matter, so does Stan."

And Stan, who had just been packing up the rest of his meeting papers, looked over, and smiled. "I heard my name."

"We're going for dinner," Dani stated. "Why don't you join us?"

Stan looked at them with interest. "You know what? That's not a bad idea. These meetings tend to wear me right out."

"Me too," Dani agreed. "Anything to do with the budget makes my skin crawl. I know we're always short on funds, and I keep looking for any influx of money to help make things meet, but I refuse to cancel the charity beds, and I refuse to cut back any more on the groceries."

Stan smiled. "And you can tell that all of us appreciate not cutting back on the groceries." He patted his stomach. "The trouble is, there really isn't any particular area that we can cut back."

"And we're holding," Dani stated firmly. "We are holding, and we're good for two more years at the rate we're going."

"And two years is a boon," he noted. "I remember when we didn't have six months locked down."

Laughing, the three of them headed toward the dining area. As Giada walked inside, the bulk of the rush was over.

Dennis still manned the front counter. When he caught sight of her, he asked, "Are you busy?"

She shook her head. "No. What's up?"

"Percy."

"Give it to me," she said. "I'll take it down right now." She turned to Dani. "Hold me a spot at the table."

Dennis passed her a large tray filled with food, and she quickly bee-lined around the railing and headed to Percy's room. The door was open, and she called out softly, "You awake?"

A mumble came from the other side of the room. As she stepped forward, she noted his eyes completely glazed in pain, staring back at her. "Oh my God." She rushed to him and placed the tray down on the small bedside table, then moved it out of the way. "Put your arm around my shoulders." His pain was bad enough from whatever position he'd slumped into that he immediately did so without argument, and she half lifted and half shoved him into a different position.

"How did you know?" he asked, gasping for breath.

She stared down to see if he were serious. "The look on your face. The pain must have been extreme."

He shrugged. "Sometimes I get back muscle seizures, but it's much better now."

She shifted the angle of the bed, until he was completely stretched out.

"Oh, that's even better." And moving his arms and legs, he stretched and rolled. "Good timing on your part."

"Now you make me feel like I should have been here earlier."

"I'm not even sure why you're here now." He sniffed the air and nodded. "Oh God, food."

"Let me see if we can get you into a better position for eating, or do you want to get up and maybe move around a bit and come down to the dining room?" she asked.

He immediately shook his head. "No, it's too early for that."

She wasn't sure what made it too early. "A wheelchair is here beside your bed. You want to sit in that to eat, and I'll lower the table?" He looked at her and looked at the wheelchair, and she could tell that was the last thing he wanted. "Keep in mind," she noted, as she brought the wheelchair around, "it really would be a complete change of position for you. Might be better for you, at least for a little while."

With that, he used her arm to sit all the way up, and afterward she shifted him into the wheelchair, so he was upright in a proper position, then she lowered the tray. "How's that?"

"This is much better. Thank you." As she turned to leave, he asked, "Who asked you to bring this?"

"I saw Dennis in the dining room. I was just joining Dani and Stan, our vet from downstairs, for dinner," she explained, "when Dennis asked if I'd bring it to you."

He looked up in surprise. "It's much appreciated."

"I'll be back after dinner," she offered, "and I'll pick up your tray for you." And, with that, she skedaddled.

PERCY STARED AT the food, but his mind was on the woman who even now raced down the hallway to meet up with the others. He used to race too, from point A to point B. He missed it. According to Aaron, Percy would get there. Even if at a funny clumping and limping run, he could still get to something a heck of a lot better than where he was right now. It was just so new to him, being here. He checked out the dinner plate—fried chicken and fried shrimp and a big veggie stir-fry. It was a bit of a jumbled menu, but it was dense in nutrition and hot and tasty. By the time he finished the second piece of fried chicken, he was almost ready to push the tray aside, but it was so good that he polished it off, right down to the end.

Resigned, he got up, grabbed the crutches, and slowly made his way to the bathroom. With his face washed, he returned and changed into his pajamas, made his way to the bed, and sat down gently. He felt like roadkill, but the full meal had helped a lot. Dessert was on the tray too, and now he thought maybe he could handle a little bit more. He had just picked up the dish of apple pie when he heard laughter in his doorway. He looked over to see Giada walking toward him.

"I just finished my piece of pie," she noted, rubbing her tummy. "I tell you, the cooks here ..."

"Well, I hope your business meeting won't cut back on the groceries," he noted, as he savored the apple pie. "Because that's the best meal I've had in months, if not years," he admitted.

"They're really good here." She surveyed his tray and looked him over. "Well, I'm glad to see the earlier spasms didn't hurt your appetite."

"I'm always hungry," he noted. "It seems like I can never get full."

"Well, that's a very good sign. Too often the medication here affects appetites, and people can't eat."

"That's not my problem," he stated, "but I have to admit I really struggled to finish this meal." He slowly replaced the empty dessert plate. She handed him the milk on the bedside table and asked, "Are you a milk drinker?"

He looked at it, frowned. "I am, but I don't know how they knew."

"I would think that your particulars would have traveled with you," she suggested.

He took a big healthy slug, draining it in one gulp, and handed it to her. She looked at the empty glass and shook her head. "It would take me two days to get through that."

"Not me. I'm an old farm boy, and milk was something that I grew up on."

"I didn't." She laughed. "My mother was into Grape-Nuts and non dairy milk. So real milk was something I never got a taste for." She picked up the tray and asked, "Now are you good to go for the moment?"

He nodded. "Do you know if I'm to expect any other people tonight?"

"Check your iPad," she noted, "for how many others on your team are left to see you. Some of them may have sent you emails too."

He frowned. "I didn't even think of that."

"If nobody is coming, and you want me to shut the door, I can also put up a sign. But it is still early, not even six."

"Oh, gosh. No, we'll leave it open for a while. Maybe some more will come tonight, and then I don't have such a busy day tomorrow."

"I just hope you have a good night," she said. "At least a full tummy will be a help." And, with that, she disappeared.

She was right in the sense that a full tummy would help, but he was also sore. That muscle spasm? He hadn't been completely honest because they'd been happening all afternoon, off and on. But when she had walked in on him, he had slowly slipped to one side and couldn't straighten on his own.

A knock came at his door not ten minutes later. Percy looked up from the iPad he'd been trying to figure out to see a man in a white lab coat.

"I'm Dr. Wilkinson."

"Nice to meet you, sir."

"I was looking over your file. Came to check on that stump of yours."

"You mean the stump that never seems to heal?" he muttered. He pulled back the blanket he had tossed over his stump and pulled up his pant leg for the doctor to take a look at it.

He gave it a good inspection and then noted, "I also heard you had some muscle spasms. And, yes, she was right to tell us," he added gently. "Do you need muscle relaxants? That trip was obviously a little rougher on your body than we would have hoped."

"It was just sitting for a long period getting here," he muttered. "It's not that bad." But the doctor wouldn't be appeased, and he gave Percy a thorough check-over.

"I'll change your medications for the night. I want you to get a good night's sleep, as that helps healing as well. Do you need anything for pain?"

Immediately Percy shook his head. "No, it's not pain anymore," he replied. "It's more stress, the muscles that won't work when I need them to work."

"Can you explain that a little more?"

He explained about trying to grab the water when Dani was here and then about the spasms earlier.

"Okay, we'll take a good look at that over the next few

days. I'll order some blood tests to see what's going on, to fix some nutritional deficiencies, along with getting some really nutritionally dense meals into you, even some green shakes maybe. Then we'll let Shane get at you."

"That sounds almost like a threat," he said, half joking.

"And some people would say Shane is a threat, but he isn't. He's all about getting you to be the best you can be," Dr. Wilkinson replied. "You're lucky to have him." And, with that, the doctor left.

And, like a typical hospital, about another hour passed when a nurse came around with a tray and medication in a small paper cup. Percy smiled as she handed it to him. The nurse said, "This will help you sleep and should calm down the muscle knots."

He nodded and took it with a little water she provided. "Am I done for the night?"

"Somebody will come back around at ten p.m. to check on you because you're a new arrival," she noted, "but, once we know that you're good to go, we won't be bugging you too many times in the night."

"Good, because it's hard to sleep if you guys keep interrupting me."

"Got it," she replied cheerfully. And she stepped away to leave.

"Wait. Is there any chance of getting a big glass of water again for the night?"

"Sure. I'll bring you back one. Flat or bubbly? Ice or no ice?"

"Flat. No ice," he stated quietly. And she disappeared. With that, he returned to his schedule on his iPad, hoping that was the end of his visitors for the night. He was ready for bed himself.

Chapter 4

THE NEXT MORNING Giada walked into her office and plunked herself down into her chair. Her brother and his girlfriend had had one humdinger of a fight at the front doorway, as she had walked in the door last night. She'd tried to disappear to give them their privacy, but that hadn't worked. They were both hot-tempered, passionate people, and Giada hoped they were in the process of making up on the front steps, but instead they'd stormed out in the backyard and kept the argument going there, before they raced back inside again to continue it.

In the meantime Giada had managed to clean up the kitchen, then made herself a cup of herbal tea and disappeared once more. Unfortunately that wasn't the end of this fight because, when Margaret left her brother, Francis had come up to talk to Giada. They talked till late into the night, and now she felt the effects. She sat down and turned on her computer, immediately craving caffeine. She'd left the house so late that she hadn't had a chance to get any yet.

With her computer on now, she picked up her mug and marched down to the dining room, only to find that breakfast was in full swing. She also hadn't eaten. Rather than getting just straight caffeine, she stepped into the buffet line and grabbed a tray. When Dennis saw her, his eyebrows shot up. "Yeah," she replied. "Believe me. I had a horrid night, no breakfast. So hit me with something that'll make me get through the day."

"Protein?"

"I'm better with fruit and yogurt," she noted, "but maybe some protein too," as she eyed the bratwurst and scrambled eggs. Dennis took note of that and loaded up a plate for her. And, still smiling, she grabbed some toast and some peanut butter and jam cups, plus a knife and fork and her coffee, and headed back to her office. She loved her job, when she could do things like eat like this on the hour. She was halfway through her breakfast when Dani walked in. Giada took one look at the cinnamon bun in her boss's hand and asked, "Where did you get that from?"

"It's not available every morning," Dani explained, "but Dennis tends to offer them every Wednesday."

"And how is it I didn't know that? I've worked here for at least eight months," she cried out.

Dani motioned at the breakfast in front of Giada. "Aren't those brats divine?"

"I've never been a big sausage person but bratwurst? Yep. they're definitely my jam," she stated.

Dani snickered at that. "It's so funny to hear you say things like that."

"Honest to God, I get it from my brother," she said, with an eye roll. "And I wish that they would just get married and stop fighting so much."

"Do you think the marriage will stop the fighting?"

"Usually the fights are about where they want to live, when they'll have children, all that kind of stuff. They need to get married and stop feeling so insecure about each other."

"You'd think at this point that the insecurity would be long gone."

"I don't know." She raised both hands, palms up, adding a bright smile, more than fed up with her brother and his relationship. "How's Percy doing this morning?"

"Better." Dani nodded. "I just spoke to him. He'll take all of today off and rest up, and we'll see how he is tomorrow."

"You think he'll make it down to the dining room for meals?"

"Well, he should get a tour sometime today, whenever he's feeling up for it. So maybe he'll eat in the dining room as part of that." Dani stepped back to the doorway, the last of the cinnamon roll popping into her mouth. She looked at her friend and asked, "Do you want to give him the tour?"

"You know what? That might not be a bad idea for both of us," Giada replied, liking the idea. "I don't get to visit with the patients enough."

"And neither do you take the time to go around the gardens either or to take advantage of our amenities." Dani walked to the doorway. "Remember. Stan says you're always welcome downstairs."

"Yeah, and that's the trouble, I guess, with not living on the property. I come in for a certain set of hours, put in my time, and then I go home. Seems like visiting with Stan and the animals just doesn't get into my schedule."

"Well, if you're caught up, today's a good day," Dani suggested. "Maybe check in with Percy around ten or eleven a.m. and see how he's doing."

"Okay, I'll do that," she noted. And Dani was gone. Giada stared out the empty doorway, wondering why Dani would have even made the suggestion. Except that staffing was always an issue, as well as a shortage of time to get everything done. Maybe because Giada had already met

Percy? It did make sense. She kept an eye on the time, and, when ten-thirty rolled around, she hopped up and walked toward his room. She knocked on the door and stepped in to see him with his iPad and a folder of paperwork.

"Surprised to see you again." Percy's face lit in welcome. "Don't you have enough work to do?"

"Well, I never see the patients enough. As much as an inventory of our stock is part of my job, so should be talking to you guys, getting feedback and ideas," she admitted. "So Dani suggested that, if you're up for it, maybe I should take you for a tour of the place."

"A tour?" he asked. "Is there really that much to show me?"

"And that's part of the problem," she admitted. "There are tons of things to see and do here, and I never get to enjoy it either."

"And how will we do that tour?"

She motioned at the wheelchair. "You're supposed to rest up today," she noted. "So I would take you around in the chair." He frowned. She gave him a winning smile. "Please, save me from having to go back to the office. I really could use some fresh air. Besides, you haven't seen the vet's office or the gardens or the horses, or the pool for that matter," she said, with a laugh.

"No, I haven't," he agreed. "Aaron did tell me about a lot of it, but I thought maybe most of it was just an exaggeration."

"From Aaron?" she asked in surprise, staring at Percy.

He shrugged. "He was working hard to get me here, so I wasn't sure how much was joking and how much was the truth."

"It's all truth," she declared. "Hop on board, MacDuff.

Let's go for a ride."

"Ha! As long as you're not taking me on a wild trip for naught," he noted.

"Did you eat breakfast this morning?" she asked.

"A tray was brought to me."

She nodded. "We'll see how you are after the tour. Maybe you'll be ready for some lunch in the dining room."

He looked at her in surprise. "Well then, maybe I should get changed. I don't want to go anywhere in pajamas."

"Sure. Do you want me to get you anything?"

He shook his head. "I've got clothing here at the end of the bed. I just hadn't bothered yet." But he got up awkwardly, grabbed the crutches and his clothing, and headed to the bathroom.

"I can step out of your room so you can get changed here."

"No, this works."

She frowned at that, wishing that she'd thought of it earlier, because she could have left and come back, but she wasn't thinking in terms of his own personal needs. And that was something that she needed to be better at. When he came out, he looked a little flushed, but he was dressed.

She noted the missing foot. "Do you have a prosthetic?"

"Not yet. The leg hasn't healed enough. And there's talk of maybe putting another layer of padding on, so I can put weight on it."

"Ah." She nodded. "All the medical intricacies that I don't understand, but, if you're telling me that it's in progress, that makes sense to me."

"It's in progress."

She burst out laughing, patted the back of the wheelchair, and said, "Let's go, soldier."

"Seaman," he corrected.

"Meaning, you're from the navy?"

"Yes," he confirmed.

"We have all kinds of military personnel here," she noted, with a laugh. "I just thought maybe *soldier* would cover it all."

"Some people would take you to task for making that kind of a mistake."

"And I just apologized," she said bluntly, "because I don't really know all the ins and outs of the different titles and ranks. Yet here everybody's the same, all patients in need of healing." She had almost said *broken* but had stopped the harsh word from coming out—blame it on her lack of sleep—but it's how she saw so many of the people here. "The good news," she added quickly—to try to cover up for her snafu when he'd gone really quiet—"is that the tools, equipment, people, and skills are here to fix them here."

"Promise?" he asked, in a low whisper.

She leaned forward and whispered against his ear, "I promise." And then she laughed and added, "And enough of that maudlin stuff. We'll start with a tour of this floor, and then we'll take you downstairs and outside. You have no idea what's coming."

"Nope," he said, with a happy sigh, "but just getting out of that hospital where I was before and getting here is a good start. I wish Aaron were here, but I get it," he murmured. "He's on to a whole new stage of life."

"He has taken on a new life," she agreed, "and, for that, I'm thrilled for him and for Dani. But that doesn't mean that you don't get to do the same. You just have to choose what direction you want to go."

PERCY STRUGGLED INTO the wheelchair, but Giada was proficient as she quickly helped him in, propped up his good leg, checked that his injured stump was comfortable, and then proceeded to push him out and down the hall. "You seem to be quite comfortable with all this," he murmured, with a slight head tilt back, so she could hear him.

"I am," she stated gently. "My brother was in a wheelchair for a long time. But he got better, and thankfully he's doing just fine now."

"Why was he in a wheelchair?"

"He broke his back, riding horses," she added, with a short laugh. "And I shouldn't laugh, but we always said that he was on the horses so often that we wouldn't be surprised if he did take a fall. He had always aspired to be a steeple-chase jockey. He was forever setting up jumps and trying them. But, of course, he did fall, and he did break his back," she shared, with a shrug. "But all's well that ends well."

He smiled, thinking about it. "How old was he?"

"Twelve," she replied.

He grinned. "So, boys will be boys?"

"That's what everybody kept saying, yes," she agreed. "He hated the wheelchair. Oh, my gosh, he hated it. But the rehab took a lot longer than normal, and he didn't get his full strength back for months."

"Interesting," Percy noted.

She pulled around a corner, and the hallway opened up to a large social common area, with a big pool table in the middle, TVs on the walls, several little seating areas.

"This is nice," he noted. "Except that it's empty."

"Of course it's empty at this time of day. Everybody is

off doing something on their schedule."

He frowned at that. "I guess I'm supposed to be too, aren't I?"

"Not today," she said, with a gentle firmness. "Not until you've recovered from your journey."

He settled back to watch, as she led him through another area. He heard dishes and talking. "I suppose it's almost lunchtime."

"It is, and we'll come back up here later." She took him over to a large bank of elevators. She pushed the button, and its huge doors opened, enough room for hospital beds and wheelchairs alike. She popped him in, stepped up beside him, and quickly the elevator dropped down a floor. "This is the floor for the vet's clinic," she announced.

When it opened, he looked to the right and saw another huge office area.

"That's where Stan and the animals are," she shared, "but we'll go this way." And she took him to the left. Up ahead were double glass doors. She led them outside, and he gave a happy sigh, as the sunshine shone directly on him. She kept walking him forward, coming to a half-covered and half-open pool deck area.

"Aaron told me a pool was here," he murmured, as he stared at the water in joy.

"It's the one thing that everybody here seems to really love," she murmured. "At least everybody I know has always been eager to get into the water."

"I wonder what's the requirement to be allowed in?"

"Funny that you should say that," she noted, "because that's almost the first question when people find out about it. I'm not sure about the timing for the pool privileges, but I presume it's individually decided. I would think water therapy would be a great healing tool, but I'm no medical expert," she added.

"Naw," he replied. "I'm quite sure that there'll be a whole lot of tests I'll have to pass before I'm allowed in there. And a hot tub too," he noted in delight, as he looked over at good-size hot tub, big enough to seat ten to twelve men.

"And it is lovely too." She didn't stop there; she kept on pushing him farther outside.

"What are all the buildings around here?" he asked curiously. Because what looked like a series of townhomes or apartments were up ahead, with another one off to the side.

"Residential housing," she noted. "Most of the staff live on the property."

He was amazed at that. "Wow, that's a huge perk. Particularly if they get the meals at the same time."

"And they do," she added, with a laugh. "I don't live on the property myself," she shared. "At the moment I'm living with my brother, but he's engaged and due to be married within six months, so I need to be making other plans."

"You don't want to live here?"

"Dani's offered to hold a place for me in six months. Yet I like living in town. It's nice to have that bit of separation between work and living, but then I also have to cook and clean at home, and I have to commute," she explained. "And that's not anywhere near as much fun as walking a few steps to work, with my meals all prepared for me."

"I would live here just for the conveniences," he suggested. "Plus, if it saves you a twenty-minute commute one way, that's about an hour a day that you don't have to deal with and that you can do something else that you like. And to not have to cook? That would be a game-changer for me."

She laughed. "And I get all that," she noted. "You're

quite right. I hadn't really considered the travel time daily. And there doesn't seem to be enough time to do anything that I want to do."

"Or is your brother hoping that you'll stay long enough for him to get married so he doesn't have to be a bachelor on his own?"

At that, she burst out laughing. When she calmed down, she added, "I think that's a big part of my brother's reticence to letting me go."

"But you don't need his permission to leave, right?"

"Nope, I just know he would prefer that I stay until his wedding."

"But maybe that's not what *you* need," Percy murmured. "Sometimes it's easier to be the one *to* leave instead of the one *who has* to leave." There was such a slight difference in the meaning, depending on how he worded it, and he tried to make his message easy for her to understand, without being insulted.

She was quiet for a long moment, and then she replied in a low tone, "Kudos to you. That's a very perceptive comment."

"You don't get to where I am in life," he stated, "without having been through a lot of hardships and seeing a lot of relationships that kind of implode just because of circumstances." He shifted his position. "You learn that so many relationships break up when they come to the major stresses in life, and honestly some of the biggest stressors are health issues."

Giada nodded. "I heard a statistic that when a woman is diagnosed with breast cancer, she is warned to get ready for a potential divorce because a lot of men—and maybe it shouldn't be just about men but maybe about a lot of partners—can't handle what'll come at them."

"Exactly," Percy agreed. "Now you take something like what I've been through, and it's way worse because there is no potentially good future ahead of me. This could be as good as it gets. Now obviously, with breast cancer, it could go either way." He hesitated. "But the whole point of this discussion is the fact that there is no guarantee in life, and some people are just not cut out to handle the tougher times. Some people never have to handle it because nobody ever gives them that opportunity. They protect them. Sometimes well past the time that they should be protected."

"Are you telling me in a roundabout way," she asked, with laughter in her voice, "that I should let my brother live on his own for a few months?"

"It would probably make him appreciate what you do for him."

"I can't say I care about that," she replied, still chuckling, "because I won't be there long-term."

"No, but what about his wife?" he asked, twisting to look up at her. "Will she appreciate the fact that he doesn't know how to do anything? Or doesn't look after himself?"

"Well, she certainly knows that he doesn't know how to do anything now," she noted. "It's a big part of their fights."

"So maybe he should have six months on his own, so that he has to step up and has to understand just what it is like to live alone, so his expectations of what his wife will do for him might then mature with him. Presuming he's not looking at sharing the household chores, given that he doesn't help you now."

"That's an interesting proposition," she murmured, frowning now. "I'm sure he would hate it. And you're right. He doesn't help. I've always looked after him."

"Of course he would hate it, but it might make him a better person."

She was quiet for a long time, and he wondered if he had somehow pushed it too far. It really was none of his business.

Yet he was interested in seeing how much people did or did not do for themselves. Granted, it was not easy to change, especially when the brother was the spoiled one, taking advantage of Giada—at least in Percy's opinion. So the brother would not want that spoiling to stop, as things would get harder on him in his life. The brother wouldn't want to endure the pain of dealing with the headache of doing something for himself, instead of having his sister take care of him.

Percy had an afterthought and shook his head. "Lots of times in therapy and in various communications sessions, like I'll be going through here, if it's possible to get away with not doing something," he explained, "most people will do everything they can to avoid that responsibility. And the harder it is to change, the more that they find ways to get out of it."

"Even though it's pertinent to their healing?"

"Absolutely," he stated, "because it's hard to change. It's hard to be responsible, especially for some people. It's hard to grow up. It's painful to change, and, when we have to do it ourselves, we must step up our education and take on the responsibility of being able-bodied again—or at least a step toward being able-bodied—and then people see us in a different light again. It's sometimes easier to stay in the shadows and to be enabled by those around us."

"Ouch," she said, softly pushing him along the path. The sunshine beat down on them. "I hadn't really expected this kind of conversation."

"And you can tell me to shut up anytime," he stated instantly. "I'm sorry. I'm really pushing boundaries here." He tilted his head up to the sky. "It's lovely outside."

"About the boundaries, not at all. It's a fascinating discussion," she admitted, "and I hadn't really considered it from my brother's viewpoint. But, of course, for him, he's always had either me or my mother looking after him."

"Why is that? Isn't he a grown man?" Percy asked.

"Yes, certainly he is. And, yes, you're right. I mean, obviously after he fully recovered from his childhood accident, he's had an easy time of it, and maybe it's been *too easy* a time of it. But I don't think he would appreciate that we're arranging his future behind his back."

"It's nothing to me." Percy let out a long whistle at the pasture and the animals in front of them. "Those horses are beautiful," he murmured, as they now passed one building and were on this gravel path. "How far does this path go?"

"All around the property down at this end. The property covers acres that are undeveloped, where Dani takes the horses for long rides, and the path doesn't go up there," she explained. "Various places are accessible to walk, even off the pathways. This is just an easy path for the wheelchair."

"It's beautiful." Indeed, Percy saw a few people walking to and from the residences as well. "I think living here would be spectacular."

"Spectacular, yes," she agreed. "I'll have to give it some thought."

"Is it something you don't personally want?"

"I didn't even think about it before now," she noted. "I do for others so much in my life that it never occurred to me to do it for myself. And," she added hurriedly, "it's not a chore or anything that I object to doing. Please don't think that."

"No, of course not," he replied. "Not part of a big Italian family by any chance, are you?"

She burst out laughing. "Absolutely I am. Although we're not so big anymore. How did you know?"

"I just know that they often take care of each other in a way that a lot of other families don't."

"Yes, and a lot of role modeling goes on too," she explained. "My mother was forever telling me to look after him."

"Of course, and you've taken it to heart, and you're still doing it."

"I am," she admitted. "Never really occurred to me to stop. I was looking forward to handing off the duty to his future wife. But it's not for six more months." She stopped at one corner of the fence. "Look at the horses here."

"Is that a llama?"

"Yep, that's a llama. There are a couple here. Also a little filly is in here somewhere, although she's getting bigger. I think six horses are here now," she noted. "And, of course, various other animals are all over the place as well. In case nobody mentioned it, we have therapy dogs, therapy cats, and an absolutely monster-size rabbit, which we bring around to visit the patients every once in a while. You're not allowed to feed any of the animals, so don't be tempted, please. Most of them are rescues and have digestive or health issues, so feeding them can compromise their own safety."

"No, I certainly won't feed them, but I would really love to see some animals again," he said wistfully. "I always had dogs growing up. You don't realize how much you miss something like that until you can't have them."

She walked just past him to face him, leaving his wheelchair where it was. "There's no reason you can't have them now, is there?"

"Well, not once I'm on my feet again," he replied, "I certainly wouldn't take on looking after a pet until I'm capable of doing it myself."

She nodded. "Plenty of animals are here. We should get back, I'll introduce you to Stan who is always looking for volunteers downstairs. So, if you ever want to connect on a non-permanent basis, yet want to help out another animal," she added, "please feel free to go downstairs and to talk to Stan. There are always animals to feed or animals that just need cuddling."

"I like the sound of that," he agreed, "and I guess Aaron, when he's completed his vet training, is coming back here, isn't he?"

"He is, indeed. He'll work with Stan, and Stan could use the help. He's pretty swamped."

"So, in other words, it's a perfect match."

"For Dani and Aaron too, I would think so. If you see the two of them together," she stated, "you'll know instinctively that it's a good match. They complement each other. When they're apart, they're both good people, and they're both fine, but you can see them glow when they're together, where they just become so much more."

"I think that's the way it's supposed to be," he said quietly.

"Sure." Giada nodded, tossing him a big smile. "Should be and are, however, are two different things."

He grinned. "What about these horses? Do you get to ride?"

"Dani does organize some rides for the staff," she replied. "We also have therapy riding sessions for the patients, if that's something that interests you—and if you pass whatever challenges Shane says that you need. You can talk to him about it."

Percy looked at the horses with interest. "It's been many years. I used to ride a lot. But I can't imagine even trying now."

"But you used to be a Navy SEAL, didn't you?"

He nodded.

"The thing is, what you used to do back then, so few people could even do at the peak of their careers," she murmured. "So even half of that will be more than most people can accomplish. I have no doubt you'll do absolutely wonderfully here."

He felt his chest swelling in joy. "I hope you mean that. I haven't been terribly good about believing Aaron. You have to understand how I've heard so many unfulfilled promises over the years that I got dulled to it."

"Understood." Giada nodded. "And you have a lot of work ahead of you, but I'm pretty sure that you'll manage."

"I'll manage," he murmured. "The question is, will it do any good?"

Chapter 5

G IADA WAS AMAZED by Percy. His insight, his thought processes, it all made her think. And not necessarily in a way that she appreciated at first because she also felt a sense of loss at the idea of leaving her brother early. As if she wanted to spend as many days with him as she could before everything changed, before the family dynamic shifted. If she were honest, Giada wasn't necessarily ready for her own version of an empty nest, but she didn't know that she could explain that to Percy. Or that it was something that she had to explain.

Percy didn't know her scenario, didn't know her brother, and she didn't really know Percy. And yet the conversation went a long way to making it feel like she was learning very quickly who he was on the inside. And Percy was a powerful man, even sitting in the wheelchair in front of her. She thought about his words as they toured the property around Hathaway House, as she showed him every place that they could get to with a wheelchair.

Then finally they returned to the main building, accessing the lower level with the clinic, seeing if Stan was about— but probably was busy, as usual—so headed toward the elevator. When Stan came out of his office and into the hallway, Giada pushed Percy over, introduced them, and explained who each man was.

Stan's face lit up. "You're Aaron's friend." Stan reached down to shake Percy's hand. "Glad to have you onboard."

"I don't know how on board I am. I was convinced to be here by Aaron."

"Of course, and that's awesome," he noted, with a smile. "Anytime you want to come on down here, feel free. The animals could always use a little attention."

"I'd like that," Percy said instantly. "It's amazing how much that helps. Both them and me."

"You guys are good for their healing too. Everybody in this world needs to know that they're loved," Stan noted quietly. "None of us are any exception to that rule." And, with that, he looked over at Giada. "How's that brother of yours doing?"

"Pretty good, getting excited about the upcoming wedding," she noted, with a big smile.

"And yet it's still months away, isn't it?"

"It sure is." Then she gave him a big eye roll. "Plans are changing on a daily basis."

"I'm sure they are. There'll be a lot of that between now and then." Stan looked at Percy. "Are you coming up to the dining room for lunch?"

She watched Percy hesitate and withdraw slightly. "Yes, he is," she replied smoothly. "I'll take him up, introduce him to the system and how it works, help him to a table with whatever his lovely food choices are, and get him back to his room afterward."

"I am kind of tired though," Percy noted.

"Yeah, which is why we'll get you back to your room right away." She could see that he didn't quite know how to get out of it. As she caught a surprised glance of Stan's, she realized that he'd seen her maneuver too. She looked over at him. "You coming up then? We'll go together."

"That's where I'm going," he said. "I'm starving. Is it a theme day?"

"I can't remember," Giada replied. "I've been so busy lately that I haven't been keeping track."

"What do you mean by theme days?" Percy asked.

"They often do meals in themes, like Greek Day, Chinese, things like that," Stan explained. "One of the best has been the Mongolian Day. Remember when they did those massive skewers of meat? Oh, my gosh, I thought I'd died and gone to heaven."

"Is the food always this good?" Percy asked curiously.

"Absolutely," Stan stated. "I swear that's why most of us live here." And he started to laugh. "That's not quite true, but obviously I'm hooked because it's my own clinic. However, the system, the way it's run here, the people we help," he noted, "it's pretty hard to find anything quite like this."

"Which is why, of course, you guys are all still here," Percy guessed.

"Exactly. I've been here almost since the beginning," he said. "And I think I hear the Major up there. If you ever get a chance to talk to that old hoot, you'll probably enjoy it too."

"Dani's Dad?"

"Yeah," Stan replied. "Have you ever met him?"

"No, but Aaron's talked about him though."

"I imagine he has. I mean, the Major will be his father-in-law, after all," Stan noted.

"That would be something to consider, wouldn't it?" Giada asked, with a laugh. "The Major is quite a character. I can't quite imagine him being family though."

"Right?" Stan nodded. "His heart is in the right place."

"I think everybody in the family has their heart in the right place," Giada added, as she pushed Percy's wheelchair back to the elevator again. "I've never seen such empathy and care and passion."

"You know what happened to her though, right?" Stan asked Giada, as he pushed the button for the elevator.

"You mean, about her father and why they started this center? I heard the rumors, but I hadn't really heard the story."

"Well, if you want to know more, you can. All you have to do is tell the Major that you haven't heard about it, and he'll be more than happy to regale you with the details. Just make sure you have an hour or two to listen."

She laughed, as she pushed Percy into the elevator. "You know what? There's something special about having family like that around, who can tell those kinds of stories too."

"Absolutely," Stan agreed. "Believe me. The Major is a character all in his own right." At that, the elevator door opened, and she pushed Percy, with Stan walking at their side, toward the buffet line.

"Oh, good, the line's not too bad yet," she stated, but then she looked out at the deck with so many of the tables full, "or maybe we're just a little bit late."

She pushed the wheelchair into the buffet line, knowing that, by Percy's silence, he must be getting more and more uncomfortable around all the other people. She grabbed a tray, put it in his lap, and said, "You hang on to that one. I'll hang on to this one."

Stan grabbed one as well. He stepped before them and said, "We'll go as a team."

As soon as Dennis saw Stan, Dennis's face lit up. Then

he realized that Percy was here too, in his wheelchair. He leaned over and said, "Percy, my man. What can I get ya?"

"What have you got?" Percy asked. "I can't even see everything yet."

"We've got fried chicken, grits, biscuits and gravy," he replied. "Plus we've got veggies and even some fried fish over here." Dennis pointed farther down the buffet line. "So, what appeals?"

"All of it?" Percy asked hesitantly. "But I need dense nutrition."

"Good," Dennis noted. "So fish or chicken?"

"Chicken. I had it before, and it's great."

"Do you want a biscuit on the side?"

Percy nodded.

"And then we'll fill the plate up with lots of veggies," Dennis added, and that's what he did.

Stan took one look at the size of the plate and said, "It's a good thing that you guys get a good work out here because, my gosh, you'd be all heavyweights if you didn't." He looked back at Dennis and stated, "I'll take half of what you just gave Percy."

"Half!" Dennis replied in outrage. "That's hardly worth shoveling onto a plate." But he followed suit, handed it off, and then turned to look at Giada. "And you, missy, what would you like?"

"How about half of what you gave Stan?" she replied, with a big grin.

"Nope, nope, nope," he argued. "You rarely eat here, so take advantage of this wonderful food. Do you want green veggies or a salad?"

"Salad," she said instantly and watched as Dennis made a fresh salad right in front of her, then asked her if she wanted dark meat or white meat from the fried chicken. By the time her plate was full, she was just as amazed at the aroma. "It smells delicious," she told Dennis, as she accepted her plate from him.

"It is. Let me come around and give you a hand." He walked over, pushing Percy forward. "Up here we've got desserts and a big drink center," he added, "so everything you could want, plus coffee and tea. What can I get you?"

Percy hesitated, then looked up at Dennis. "How about just water for now? Maybe a cup of tea and a dessert after I have plowed through this."

"Good call," Dennis noted.

Giada watched as Dennis maneuvered Percy right out onto the deck, where already a good thirty or forty other people were already seated. "Do you want sunshine or shade?"

"Sunshine, if it isn't too-too bright," Percy replied. At that, Dennis moved him to a large umbrella-covered table. "You pick whereabouts you want to sit at the table. You can get a little sun or a lot here." And then he set down the tray Percy carried and said, "I'll be back with water."

She pulled up beside Percy and sat down next to him. "See? It's quite the place." He looked at her, and she saw Percy's stunned amusement.

"No wonder Aaron doesn't want to leave. This place is very special."

"Yeah, they do like to take exceptional care of their pa-tients and their staff," she noted, with a grin. "And we do argue about budgets all the time."

"No wonder," he said. "I can't imagine keeping it run-ning at this level of quality is easy."

"Not easy," she agreed, "but important. Food is to feed

and to help nurture and to heal. If you don't have good quality food," she says, "it won't help you guys get back on your feet."

The look on his face when he bit into the fried chicken moved her in a way she hadn't expected, with such a sense of peaceful joy, as he sat here and just slowly worked his way through the chicken leg in his hand. She stopped eating to watch.

Finally Stan nudged her gently. "You should be eating your own food."

She looked down at her chicken. She took a bite, and it was wonderful, no doubt about it. But to see somebody enjoy it in the same way that Percy had was just incredible. When he sat back and stared at the second piece of chicken still on his plate, he looked over at her and said, "I haven't had anything this good in so very long," he whispered.

"Enjoy it," she replied gently. "It won't disappear off your plate, but we don't offer fried chicken every day. The menu changes on a regular basis." He was such a sensual man that it really surprised her and made her feel odd, as if it were a private experience to watch as he thoroughly enjoyed his food. She was done in half the time, and it reminded her that she'd gotten into the habit of just eating because food was in front of her, yet not taking the time to slow down and to enjoy it.

Percy looked over at her plate. "You must have been hungry."

"I was," she admitted. "But you're a good reminder that I need to slow down and to enjoy my food more."

He nodded enthusiastically. "Good God, if you've eaten the swill that I've eaten for the last year, you would not be rushing through this. This is almost like a ..." He didn't even know what to say. "But it's, … it's almost like an intimate experience. And I know that sounds weird, but it's just so nice to enjoy good food again."

"I get it. You keep enjoying. I'll go grab a coffee." She got up, needing to put a little time and distance between him and her. She rushed over to get drinks. Stan waited until she got back, and then he excused himself. She put a cup of coffee down in front of Percy. "It might be a bit too early for you," she noted, "but I was already there." She sat down beside him. "Wow. You're almost done."

"Well, I sped it up a little bit," he admitted. "I just seemed to be taking too long."

"No," she replied, "don't ever feel that way. The good thing is that you're taking the time to enjoy your food. Whereas I just rush through mine too often."

"Nothing quite like having terrible food for a long time to make you appreciate it when you get something so much better."

She laughed. "And I don't spend enough time here to get to appreciate the food here very much. I go home and look after my brother." Percy didn't say anything, but she felt almost a sense of him withdrawing again. She smiled. "And you made some really good points about my brother. I'll consider them."

He looked at her in surprise. "You need to do you," he replied, "not what I say."

"Oh, I wouldn't do it because of that," she murmured. "But you did make some valid points that I should consider, and it is something that I will consider," she murmured. "If nothing else, I have to also consider him."

"Good point." Percy pushed away his tray. "My God, I need to go sleep for an hour," he murmured.

"You know something? That's one of the advantages

here. You can do that," she said, with a gentle smile. "You get to go back, relax, and digest everything that you just put into your stomach."

"Yeah, but, at one point in time," he noted, "I'm supposed to start work. Aaron's warned me that it won't be easy to get where I want to go."

"Maybe not," she agreed. "But"—as she stood up and removed his tray, so that the mess wasn't in front of him anymore—"it will be worth it."

TALK ABOUT SURPRISED when she'd shown up with the promise of a tour. But a good surprise for Percy. Giada brought sunshine into his life every time he saw her. A lovely feeling but one he wasn't used to. Neither was he used to worrying about someone else since his accident, but he found her situation odd and her reaction harder to forget.

Was her brother a serious danger to her or were Percy's instincts just on overdrive, having seen so much of the ugliness in the world throughout his naval career? Still he had to trust that she knew her brother and that she knew how to handle him.

Lunch had left Percy tired. Yet he had shooed Giada back to her real work, promising that he could make it to his room on his own. Maybe a nap wouldn't be a bad idea. He pushed away from the table and slowly made his way to his bed. At least it might help him to disconnect from Giada's situation and to help him refocus on his own healing. He was meeting with Shane in an hour for some testing, so any break Percy could catch now he needed to take.

He lay down on his bed and was asleep in minutes.

Chapter 6

WHEN PERCY'S TRAINING started, it started with a vengeance. Giada heard about it throughout the next few days, as she stopped in to see him once, while he went through a workout with Shane. According to Percy, he had testing first, alignment next, then treatment plan after that. When she walked by his room two days later in the evening, he was in bed, once again pinched with a muscle cramp. She raced over, gasping, "Not again." He gave her half a smile, as she straightened him up. "Did you talk to Shane about this?"

"Yes, it's part of what we were working on first," he said, with an eye roll. "I don't know how anybody thinks they'll fix this."

"Leave it to Shane," she replied immediately. She frowned, studying him. "You're still in a lot of pain. Do you want a nurse?" He just glared at her for that suggestion. "Muscle relaxants then maybe?"

"Well, a trip to the hot tub would be nice, or the pool. Other than that? I'll just stay here and wait until the pain recedes."

"If you say so," she replied, retreating. As she stepped out of his room, she immediately headed for Shane. As she walked into his office, he was on the phone.

He held up a finger, asking her to wait, and, by the time

he had logged off the call, he turned to her with a bright smile and asked, "Hey, how are you?"

"I just came from Percy," she said, without preamble. "I'm really worried. This is the second time he was in a complete muscle spasm and twisted to the side." She demonstrated.

"He told me about those." Shane rose, grabbing his iPad. "Yet I've never yet seen that in progress."

"I hope he never has one again," she noted. "He looked like he was in screaming pain, yet he refuses any suggestion of medication."

"Right, he's quite against any kind of painkillers."

"I know. I asked if I could get him a nurse, but he just shot me a nasty look."

Shane laughed. "Yeah, these guys come in here pretty tough, and it takes a lot to knock them. Some are very against drugs, taking too many or taking any."

"I get it," she noted, "but he really didn't look very good."

"I'll go see him now."

"He did suggest the hot tub or the pool."

Shane looked at her in surprise. "It's pretty early yet."

"He's in a lot of pain. I don't know what's going on with that weird horizontal pull, but it looks pretty agonizing."

"Okay, I'm on it. Thanks for the heads-up." He stopped, looked at her, and asked, "Are you on your way home now?"

"I am. I'll check on him in the morning."

He grinned. "I see he's gotten under your skin, huh?"

"It's hard not to like somebody like that," she said. "We hit it off right at the beginning, and, after that, it's just kind of, I don't know. I'm always worried about him." She shrugged, for lack of a better answer.

"And that's a good thing," Shane murmured. "I don't think he's had a whole lot of people look after him. Or even care if he made it."

"And how is that even a thing?" she asked in disgust. "I mean, my brother doesn't need the care I give him, but I don't know how people cannot look after those who they love."

"Sometimes they just aren't equipped to receive love," Shane murmured. "I've known quite a few family members who couldn't be around their loved ones because it tore them apart."

"Oh, I hadn't considered that," she replied. "I mean, that still seems kind of selfish to not be there while somebody is going through treatment, when you think about it."

"People are all different," Shane noted, "and we've seen all kinds here. It might be selfish to you, but, for them, maybe they think that because they can't control their emotions and they might hate themselves for it, they're better off elsewhere, in order to have their loved one do better without them. Because once a loved one finds out that somebody else is suffering, you know it impacts their ability to do their best and to look after themselves." Shane shook his head. "This is all about the patient. It's not about those around them."

"No, you've got a good point there. I'll have to think about that." She stopped on her way out, as she headed down the hallway, still walking backward. "Have you talked … have you ever had a serious discussion with him, like a philosophical one? He's got quite some things to say," she noted. "His whole belief system, or at least his way of thinking, is unique. It's so interesting to have a conversation with him."

"I'll try. I'll see about that," he said. "So far, it's just been about the training. And I'm always the bad guy when it comes to that."

She rolled her eyes. "I wouldn't want your job just for that reason alone."

"Yeah, you just get to tell all of us that we can't have toilet paper in our bathrooms because we're using too much." And, with that, he burst out laughing and headed toward Percy's room.

SLOW BREATHING. SLOW breathing. If ever anything could get Percy's balance back, it would be that. At least that's what everybody else had told him. Nobody seemed to care about what Percy said to them. When he heard footsteps, firm and heavy, walking toward him, he winced. With his luck, Giada had immediately run to Shane and told him about the problems Percy was having.

When Shane popped his head through the door a moment later, Percy knew he was right. Shane frowned at him, and Percy frowned right back. "She just couldn't resist telling you, huh?" he muttered, hating the sense of just not being fully honest with himself as to how it felt being a victim to his body, being paralyzed by what was happening, being unable to handle any of this. "I shouldn't get mad at her," he admitted. "But it feels very much like I'm at the mercy of my body right now, and I don't like it."

"Of course not," Shane agreed. "I would suggest the hot tub."

At that, Percy stared at Shane in shock. "Seriously?

Don't joke with me, man, because that would be nirvana right about now."

"In that case, let's make that happen." Shane walked over to the closet and asked, "Do you have swimming shorts?"

"No. I. … Well, I don't know, maybe."

Shane went through his stuff. "Yep, you got one pair here. Which is good."

"Yeah, it's probably in the stash Aaron left for me."

"Maybe," Shane replied. "Doesn't matter where they came from, as long as they're clean and you're good to wear them. I suggest we don't look a gift horse in the mouth."

"Right now," Percy admitted, "I'd probably put on a woman's bikini, if it meant getting in the hot tub."

Shane burst out laughing. "Any other day, I might take you up on on that."

He grinned. "Oh, please don't, but, if that doesn't tell you how desperate I am right now, nothing will."

"Oh, it says a lot, but I didn't need it. I see the look on your face. That's why I'm here. And that's why Giada came and told me."

"Right." With Shane's help, Percy got switched into his swimming shorts. And Shane almost lifted him fully to transfer him to the wheelchair, then grabbed a big towel. "Let's go." The trip downstairs seemed to take forever, but at the same time it was fast; he knew that. "You made that trip in no time."

"Yep, I did, indeed, but then I've been doing this trip quite a few times. I know how fast the wheelchairs can go. And I'm not a young woman, like Giada, without a ton of upper arm strength. Believe me. When I want this wheel-chair to go someplace, it'll go."

"I miss that," Percy admitted quietly. "I miss knowing that, when I flex a muscle, it'll do what I tell it to do and that I can count on it being there for me when I need it to be," he murmured.

"And we can get that back for you," Shane stated. "This is a process. The end result is your health, as good as we can get it. I know it's trite to say, *Trust in the process and remember to enjoy the journey*, but really you do need to remember that, especially in your case."

"Why in my case?" he asked in surprise.

"Because a lot of the damage is not just in one or two locations. You have damage throughout your system," he noted. "So, even as we work on one area, and we recruit various muscles to help, those muscles need other muscles to help and must have other muscles recruited to make them work. This is a process. You won't see progress for a very long time, and then you'll start to see improvement."

It took a while to digest what Shane was really saying. "How long is a long time?" Percy muttered.

"It could be six months," Shane stated. "You're here for a long time. Enjoy it because I can't speed it up, and speeding it up means taking shortcuts."

"I don't want any shortcuts," Percy replied quietly. "I just want to trust that, when I take a step, that step's there."

"And that's what I'll do," he noted, "but because you've got damage on both sides of the body—and top and bottom, and front and back—I can't just say, *Okay, we'll fix just your leg because that's all that needs fixing.*" Shane shook his head. "It's not that simple with you. And, no, it probably won't be a full six months, but, if you think about it as being six months, then, when it's three months, you'll be happy. If I tell you three months, and it takes four and a half, you'll get angry."

"Right," Percy agreed, "so it's psychological."

"It's always, *always* psychological," Shane declared in a firm voice. "You have to beat the depression. You have to beat the mood swings. You have to beat the jealousy. You have to beat the highs one moment and the absolute pain of defeat the next," Shane explained. "It is all psychological. I don't care what anybody tells you. They're lying if they tell you that your mind isn't as important as everything else. So keep that at the forefront, as we work through the process. You'll get there, but nobody promised you that it would be a picnic."

I know," Percy stated. "I already thought that I was through the worst of it though. And now having the testing today?" He shook his head, almost wordless. "And I should have thought that the testing might have brought this on, yet I wasn't thinking the testing was that bad or that we had pushed the testing that far. So that's my fault."

"Your fault?" Shane shook his head. "Nobody could blame you for this. No," he repeated. "I didn't give you anything for a muscle relaxant either."

"And I wouldn't have taken it," Percy replied bluntly. "I've had just enough poor responses to those that I don't generally take them."

"What do you mean by poor responses?"

"My system doesn't like them. I can get diarrhea for days if I take them. Migraines, stomach cramps, you name it. And believe me. When you're already broken and stuck in a bed, diarrhea is not anything that you wish on anybody else who has to lie there in a bed and get help with the basics of bodily functions," he noted bitterly.

"Got it," Shane replied. "However, there are different

kinds."

"And we tested, I think, every one out there. Not fun."

"Good enough. Hot tub it is."

"Hot tub sounds perfect."

"Have you ever tried it though?" Shane asked, as he led his patient to the edge of the pool. It was late afternoon, and people were around. "I didn't even think that it would be busy now. The hot tub's for everyone, particularly after hours," he noted. "But, if I need to shanghai it, believe me. I will."

"I don't want to chase everybody else out if they're having fun," Percy said, twisting to see the hot tub area. "But it doesn't look like it's very full, is it?"

"No, and I think they're leaving actually."

Percy turned to see a group of women and one guy step out of the hot tub and head over to towels. "Are they leaving because of me?" he asked in a hushed voice.

"I don't care if they are or not," Shane stated bluntly. "Patients first always."

"I know, but …" And then Percy stopped and shrugged. "Well, I guess they're already out now anyway."

"Exactly," Shane agreed. "You forget about them. You worry about you." And, with that, Shane pushed him to the side of the hot tub, put the brakes on the wheelchair, and asked, "Can you get out on your own? And be careful because this is slippery. I didn't bring your crutches, so use my arm."

"I think I might be okay."

Shane shook his head. "Don't be stubborn. A fall on the tiles is not for anybody. And, as much as I can pick you up and put you back in that wheelchair, I would have to then rethink your ability to go in the hot tub."

He glared at Shane. "That's blackmail."

Shane gave him a wolfish smile. "Whatever works."

Percy groaned, used Shane's arm to help pull himself up, and, with his other hand, he used the railing and slowly lowered himself into the tub, feeling the warm water on his injured stump as he slid lower into the water, almost shuddering in delight. "Dear God, how is it that the heat and the water can feel so good?"

Feeling the heat slowly seeping into his bones, he let his body relax fully, sinking under the water, including his face. He lay at the bottom of the hot tub and just shifted slightly enough to note that the pain had eased. When he surfaced, Shane stood in the hot tub beside him. "I'm fine. Much better, in fact."

"That's good to know," Shane replied, "but we'll run through a couple exercises to loosen up those muscles. We'll work on the opposite side of your body, but that side's also damaged, right? Remember that. So we'll have to recruit other muscles to help."

And the exercises that followed were ones Percy had never done before, but he felt the tension and the stiffness of the muscles easing by the time he was done. Twenty minutes later, Shane had him standing and effectively doing a variation of jumping jacks in the water. Which, considering he only had one foot, was a feat in itself, but, also considering that he was in water, it was doable. "Interesting," Percy said, when they were done. "I feel better."

"Now twist to the side." With those words, Shane quickly demonstrated the move himself.

"That feels very much like a yoga twist," Percy protested.

"Whatever works," Shane said. "Remember. This isn't about right or wrong. It's about what works for you."

"Got it." Finally he sank back into the water. "Just even the heat helps."

Shane nodded. "There's something very healing about water and heat, isn't there?"

"Absolutely." He looked up at the balcony area off the dining room. "I guess it's dinnertime, and that's why everybody's up there?" And, indeed, the balcony was full.

"Yep, sure is," Shane agreed, "but I don't want you worrying about getting up there for a meal."

"That's good, because, honest to God, I wouldn't make it. But I am hungry."

"Hunger is good, particularly after what you've been through," Shane noted. "Too often the appetite turns off, and you don't want to eat when you're in so much pain."

"Well, the pain's eased now," he said, "but how am I supposed to get food, especially when I'm soaking wet?"

"You don't worry about it. I'll get you some."

"You're wet too."

He shrugged. "And that again is not an issue. I've got shoes and socks and a towel here. I'll dry off, go up, and get you a meal."

"And I can eat it in the hot tub?" he asked in surprise.

"As long as you promise to not dip your food in the hot water, like a two-year-old. Yeah, we're adults here. You'll do the best you can to keep food out of the hot tub, and we'll do the best we can to get you back on your feet." With that Shane hopped out, dried off his feet, and said, "I'm not even sure what's on tap today. Any suggestions about what you would like?"

"Honestly I'm really hungry now, so I don't care what it is, just make sure it's lots."

"Got it." Shane turned and headed up the stairs toward

the dining room.

Unbelievable to think that Percy was here now at this stage of his life in a hot tub, staring up at the beautiful Texas sky, waiting for somebody to bring him a hot meal. What had happened to his world? This would never have been his life in the VA centers. Yet he knew that the veterans' centers were great for running a lot of people through at a fast pace. Kind of like public school. It was good for a lot of people, herding them through the channels that they needed to be herded through, but, for the people who didn't quite fit or for the people who didn't do well in that kind of a system, it wasn't very good at all.

But you'll never convince anybody that something had to change. It seemed like the lobbyists and the government officials just didn't get it. Or maybe they did get it, and it was a case of it just didn't matter to them. The numbers mattered, and whatever had to be done to get the majority through a system was what they would go with.

And maybe if Percy were a bureaucrat, he would understand it himself. But, being on the other end of that, well? That was a whole different story. And he was so very grateful to be here, even though it may not be for the same reasons that Aaron had shared. Still, Percy was grateful right now at this moment to be here.

He closed his eyes and just let himself relax.

Chapter 7

GIADA COULDN'T LEAVE at the end of the day. She kept rehearsing what her excuse was to herself but finally gave in. "Okay, I can't leave until I know he's okay."

She marched down to Shane's office, only to find he wasn't there. Worried, she raced to Percy's room, only to find it empty. Now she was really stumped. She turned and looked up and down the hallway and caught sight of Dani.

Dani raised an eyebrow. "Problems?"

"I don't know," she replied. "I guess not, but … I stopped in to see Percy earlier, and he was in terrible pain, so I got Shane to help him. Now neither of them are here."

"Shane may have taken Percy to the gym."

"He did mention the hot tub, but I don't think that was on tap for him. Shane told me that it was generally too early for that."

"Shane makes those decisions on the fly," Dani noted, "depending on the immediate circumstances. Go out on the deck and look over. You never know."

"I don't want to intrude."

"Oh, I don't think it's intruding to show that you care about somebody," Dani noted.

Giada flushed. "Well, I mean …" Then she gave up her excuses yet again. "Okay, I know. It's stupid, but I find myself gravitating toward him."

"And that's a good sign," Dani noted, with a gentle smile. "He's a nice guy."

"I know he is a nice guy. I just … it feels strange. Usually the only person I'm worried about is my brother."

"I don't think your brother really needs to be worried about anymore," Dani stated, chuckling.

"And yet somehow I still find myself in the position of a mother hen," she muttered.

"And that's because you come with a big heart, and now that your brother will be off on his own and doing well, just make sure you're not looking for another project," Dani suggested, with a slight warning.

"*Hmm*. I never really considered my brother a project."

"And I'm sure you'd never consider having a relationship as being a project either," she admitted. "But us mother hens have a tendency to collect people around us who need help. Maybe, for a time, you need somebody who doesn't need help."

"I don't even think it's that. I think it's just my nature," she explained, with a smile. "Even when I was little, I was always patching up people and making them feel better and bringing them tea."

"And that," Dani noted, "is a joy because that just means you come from a good heart."

"I would like to think so," she said.

"Then go check the dining room and look over to see if they're in the hot tub. Who knows? They could even be in the pool."

"Maybe I'll take a quick look," she stated, "and then I'll … I'll head home."

"Or you could stay for dinner and maybe make sure that he gets some food too."

"Shane would see to that, wouldn't he?"

"Sure he would, but you don't know where Shane's at right now."

Giada wasn't sure whether Dani was being deliberately manipulative, trying to get Giada closer to Percy or not. The trouble was, Dani had piqued enough interest in Giada that she wanted to ensure Percy was okay. She headed to the dining room and, sure enough, from the railing, could see Percy and Shane down below, both of them in the hot tub. She watched the two of them as they talked, did a bunch of exercises, and then Shane hopped out. She was at the top of the stairs when Shane came up.

He took one look at her and said, "You couldn't leave without making sure, huh?"

She shrugged. "He was in a lot of pain," she replied in a low voice.

Shane smiled gently. "Hey, when you're here as much as we are, it's easy to become attached to people and to worry about them. And it was a good thing that you contacted me, but, as you can see, Percy's doing much better."

"I'm glad to see that." She shrugged. "It is a relief."

"I'm about to get him some food, so he can eat it at the hot tub."

"Can he do that?" she asked. "Like, wow. Never occurred to me that that would be a thing."

"Well, it's not exactly something that we encourage, but he's relaxing, and his muscles are doing fine right now. So I'd just as soon he spends a few more minutes in there, rather than panicking about getting dressed and getting up for a meal, before it's over."

"Oh, I didn't even think about that. I guess things like that are a stress for people who struggle to get where they need to be on time, isn't it?"

"It is, indeed," Shane agreed, "and stress management is key—for our patients and our staff. We do everything we can to minimize it."

"You're a good person, Shane," she said impulsively.

He looked at her in surprise. "You're just now finding that out?"

Her laughter pealed free. "Oh, my. I didn't mean it that way. It's just this place here always surprises me with how human everyone is."

"Remember that," he noted. "We're all human, and that's both good and bad. Now I'll get some food for him. Any idea what he wants?"

"I'll come with you," she offered. "I was trying to remember the things that he said he liked, but I don't remember anything he didn't like."

"That's what he told me. *Just make sure it was lots.*"

"Sounds about right," she agreed. "He does seem to have a good appetite."

"And that's the best thing ever," Shane murmured. "We need nutrients, and food is the easiest and most enjoyable way to get them."

"But you have to get lots that way."

"Hence the nutrient-dense foods," he noted, "and often we work with the kitchen to ensure that there is always a balance of nutrients in the meals."

She nodded. "The food they produce is magnificent."

Shane grinned. "Dennis is very good at maneuvering healthy plates full of food for everyone."

"He is kind of amazing, isn't he?" she noted, as they stepped into line.

At that, Dennis looked over and asked, "Who's amazing?"

She immediately answered, "You are."

He batted his huge eyelashes at her. "Glad you finally noticed."

She chuckled. "We're here to get food for Percy."

"Again?" he asked. "He won't make it in?"

"He's soaking in the hot tub," she said, with a grin.

"Well, what are you doing out here then? You should be in the hot tub with him."

She immediately shook her head. "I should be at home. We're just here to get food for him. Shane wasn't exactly sure what he would like."

"*Uh-huh*. Well, Shane could have asked me too, you know?" Dennis mentioned, grinning.

She looked over at Shane, who just shrugged and admitted, "I probably could have. Didn't think of it."

But his answer was a little too glib. She, once again, wasn't sure if they were maneuvering her into something or not. But she decided to ignore it.

"So what do you suggest for him?" Shane asked.

She looked down at the food. "Oh, my God, you have Yorkshire puddings."

"Yep, and we've got prime rib to go with those Yorkshire puddings, plus gravy, mashed potatoes, the whole works."

"He wants it all," she replied instantly. "And I mean *all* of it."

"You got it," Dennis stated. "And I probably would have agreed with that too. Percy looks like he's a big eater, who likes his home-cooked meals."

"Absolutely," she agreed, her mouth watering at the smells. When Dennis served up two big plates and handed them over, she looked at them and turned toward Shane.

"This one's for you, Shane."

Shane shook his head. "Nope, sure isn't. That's one for you and one for Percy."

"Oh, no, I've got to go home and feed my brother."

"That brother of yours does not need to be fed. He's an adult, about to become a married man," Dennis argued, with a shake of his head. "Percy, on the other hand, needs to be perked up. He's had a rough day."

Instantly she nodded. "He has, hasn't he?" But she remained torn. And, with two plates on one tray, it was very full.

Dennis noted that and shuffled her plate to a second tray. "Now that's your tray, and I've got his. What else does he want here?" And he kept her moving through the buffet line, as they added to both plates. By the time she was at the end of the line, she stared down at the ladened tray. "I feel like you did that on purpose."

"You have to move fast in this place," Shane noted. "Before you know it, Percy will be snapped up by somebody else, and you will have lost your chance."

She looked at him and gasped. "You are matchmaking," she cried out.

He laughed and laughed. "Heck no. I'd never do something like that, but Dennis on the other hand? Now Dennis would."

She turned to look behind Shane, but Dennis was busy with the next person already.

"Besides, you can't turn away from all this good food," he added. "Plus, Percy really would appreciate the company. I was hoping to have mine with my pretty lady."

"Oh my. Yes, of course. I'll stay and have dinner with Percy," she replied. "Maybe you can deliver one of these trays, and I'll stay with him at the hot tub."

"And then I'll come for him afterward," Shane noted. "I did bring him in the wheelchair, and I don't think he'll have the energy to get out of the hot tub alone, much less back up here."

"Okay," she agreed. "How long before you'll be back?"

"I'm having dinner with Melissa. How about I come in forty-five minutes?" he asked, with a raised eyebrow.

Giada nodded. "That should work." And she wouldn't be too-too late getting home then. She'd still have time to make her brother something for dinner. And, even as she thought about it, while working her way down the stairs carefully with her tray in hand, she had to wonder at the wisdom of even doing that tonight.

Dennis was right. Her brother should be looking after himself and, in theory, was perfectly capable of doing so. He just didn't particularly like to. But, as she had told the guys quite happily, she didn't have much longer to keep doing this, so whatever. Yet, in some ways, six months started to look like a very long time. Even if she did move out, early or not, where would she move to?

When she looked at the food on her tray and the beautiful grounds around her, Giada wondered if she really had any good reason to *not* ask Dani about lodging here. And maybe sooner than six months from now.

As she looked down at Percy, completely floating on his back in the hot tub, she realized that he would be here for at least that long, if not longer. Not that she had seen all the patients rehabbed by Hathaway House, but she recognized when a lot of work was to be done. And, with any luck, Percy would be as good as new when he left here. But, until then, it would take a lot to keep him on the straight and narrow.

And she didn't want another "project," but, at the same time, somebody like him? Well, he was worth the effort. She made her way across to the hot tub. She stopped and said, "Hello."

Percy opened his eyes and immediately scrambled backward.

"I didn't mean to disturb you." She turned, as Shane stepped up beside them. She explained, "I don't know if it's okay with you, but Shane and I brought dinner for you. And I thought I'd join you."

Percy stared at her, and a slow smile dawned across his face. "I will never say no to the company of a beautiful woman," he murmured.

"And I'll never say no to the presence of an almost naked man in front of me having dinner either," she teased, with a chuckle.

He burst out laughing.

Even Shane grinned, when he placed the tray down. "I'll be back in forty-five minutes to collect both of you." And, with that, he was gone.

WHEN HE WOKE the next morning, Percy realized he'd had his first decent night's sleep in a very long time. He hesitated to move in case it triggered spasms, like before. But, as he slowly shifted, his movements extremely careful, he felt no pain, no twitches, no spasms, no nothing. Emboldened, he tried again and slowly pushed himself up, sitting on the edge of the bed. Still no pain. Eyebrows up, he managed to make his way to the bathroom, and, sure enough, he made it all the way without cramping up. He wasn't sure if it was the hot tub or the testing or the interest of a beautiful woman or what it was, but he was forever grateful for it.

He'd be sure to tell Shane, when he got a chance. And given today would be more of the same—at least so Percy thought—he figured he wouldn't have to wait very long for that opportunity.

Determined to have a better start to his day, knowing some people would say he should leave well enough alone, he managed to get dressed and into his wheelchair and slowly wheeled his way to the dining room for breakfast, realizing already that that much exertion might have been a little bit too much. But, hey, he was committed now, and it was pretty hard to get anywhere without that commitment here.

As he slowly meandered, several other people walked past, saying, *Hi, Good morning*, various other comments to Percy, talking to each other and to some other people he couldn't see, presuming that they were talking on the phone. By the time Percy reached the dining area, he felt sweat on his forehead. Not good. He was already physically stressed, and that wouldn't help. He slowly pushed himself up to the front counter. Dennis took one look and beamed.

"Well, I'm glad to see you here, kiddo," he greeted Percy. "But the fact of the matter is, it looks like it was a bit too much, too soon."

Percy nodded, his breath coming out in gasps. "It probably was," he agreed. "You think you're doing okay, and then you try something and realize that you really should have just stayed in bed."

Dennis laughed. "Well, you're here. We'll get you set up with a nice breakfast, and then, if you need help going back," he stated, "I can give you a hand."

"But you've got a whole kitchen to run." Percy waved his hand at the full tables all around the room and even outside.

"Doesn't matter to me none," Dennis stated. "We'll see how you feel after you've eaten a good breakfast and sat and rested for a while. Then, if needed, I'll get you back safe and sound. Don't you worry."

And Percy believed Dennis. Percy didn't know why, but just something was very good-hearted about this man. As Percy pushed his way forward, his stomach grumbled.

"Sounds like your body is looking for food."

"Since getting here, smelling all this tempting food, I'm ravenous."

"And that's good," Dennis stated firmly. "What can I get you?"

By the time Dennis had served Percy, he had a full plate stacked up on a tray, with coffee, water, and juice on it. He just now realized that he wasn't sure he could maneuver all this in his chair and make it successfully to a table. If he placed the tray on his lap, it would be almost impossible to keep the juice and the coffee from spilling. Then he felt a gentle hand on his shoulder.

"Can I give you a hand with that?"

Surprised, he looked up to see Giada. "How come you're always here when I need you?" he asked a little crossly. "I was really trying to be independent today."

"Well, if I was the one in the wheelchair," she noted, "I wouldn't know how to get that full tray to a table. It's either carry it with your hand and somehow get your legs to do the job or put it in your lap and then coating your eggs in coffee."

He burst out laughing. "I was just considering that decision—which I would sacrifice—when you found me," he admitted.

She grinned and took his tray from his hands. "I'm not sure what the technique is around here, but I'm sure somebody can show you. In the meantime, how about I take this, and you tell me where you're planning on sitting?"

"Well, I was planning on sitting," he replied, with half a leer, "wherever this beautiful woman I talked to last night was sitting."

"I have about ten minutes before work starts," she noted, "but those ten minutes are yours. So where will it be?"

They settled on outside on the balcony. When he finally got there, he felt a sense of satisfaction but also fatigue. "It's harder than it looks," he admitted.

"And I thought you were doing wonderfully," she stated in a firm tone of voice.

"And there's that cheerleader in you again," he said, with a head shake.

"Doesn't matter if it is cheerleading or not. I'm not lying," she noted firmly.

"Good. I would hate to think that's something that you would do."

"No, I don't have time for it," she explained. "Life is for living, and it really is for people who get up and do. The rest of the world sits back and lets every day go by, as if it's meaningless."

"How come you're so focused on going forward?"

"Lately I'm not even sure that I am," she noted quietly. "But I've been kind of looking after my brother for a very long time. Well past the point that I should be."

"How old's your brother?"

She winced. "Thirty."

He looked at her in surprise. Nothing else to do but stare, as he composed his thoughts so he wouldn't alienate her in one sentence. "And you're looking after him?" He was at a loss for words. So was she, it seemed. Hesitantly knowing they'd spoken of her brother earlier but needing to make sure, Percy asked, "Is he sick or disabled?"

"No, he's not disabled," she replied crossly. "He's spoiled. He's getting married in six months, and that's now become another problem."

"Well, he's had a built-in maid and housekeeper for how long? Why would he want to change that status quo now?" he asked curiously.

"Obviously he doesn't. And I'm the fool who let it get this far."

"I don't know that you're a fool, not when you do anything outta love," he stated quietly. "Your brother's a very lucky man."

"I don't think he believes that," she replied, with a grin.

"That's just because he's stuck in his own head at the moment. I'm surprised he found somebody, if he's as dependent on you as it sounds."

"I don't think he's told her how dependent he is. They do argue about it, but I'm still not sure she fully understands. And that'll be a problem, once they are married."

"Yes," he agreed, "but it's not your problem."

She looked at him in surprise. "And you're not the first person to tell me that I either," she admitted begrudgingly. "But it's quite hard to let go, when it's been me and him all this time."

"I get it," Percy agreed cheerfully. "You're a mother hen."

"Am I?" she asked, staring at him, fascinated. "How

would you know?"

"I can see it," he murmured. "And again that's not a bad quality, but, like every hen, they know when their offspring needs to live on their own. And when that dependency has become too much, even for her."

"Not sure that it's become too much for me," she argued, "but I accept that part of the blame is my own."

"No blame," he murmured. "Your brother's thirty, well past the point in time of needing anybody to be blamed for his behavior. He's comfortable being spoiled. And *comfortable* isn't necessarily good for his emotional growth."

"No, it probably isn't," she confessed. "Dani did offer me a place here. I ... I've been wondering lately if I shouldn't take her up on it."

"Six months of living alone will make him a much better man," Percy murmured. "You might want to think about that from a motherly perspective, even from his fiancée's perspective."

"He won't like you one bit," she stated, chuckling.

"Nope, not likely," he agreed, "but then, just as we have some plain truths here in my world, there should be a few plain truths in your brother's world too."

"And in mine," she noted, with a knowing gaze at Percy. "I have to let go."

"Well, you'll let go one way or the other," he pointed out quietly, "in six months. Why would you let it get that bad, and why would you make the pain that much worse by dragging it right out to the end?"

"I get it," she replied thoughtfully. She looked up to see Shane approaching. "Oops, here's the boss, and I need to go." She hopped up, looked down at Percy. "I hope tonight is better than the last few days have been for you."

"They haven't been bad," he clarified. "They've just been tough."

"And you are one tough cookie. You've got this," she stated, with a bright smile. And, with that, she was gone.

Chapter 8

G IADA RACED TOWARD Dani's office. She'd seen her boss and friend exit the dining room and realized that she really did need to see whether a residence here was an option or not. As she reached her boss's doorway, Dani was just sitting down with a big cinnamon bun. "You must be some kind of busy around this place in order to wear off those cinnamon buns."

"Thankfully I have no trouble keeping busy here." Dani laughed. "Unfortunately it's too busy."

"I know," Giada agreed. She stepped inside Dani's office and asked, "So is your offer of a residence serious?"

"Let me take a look and see what we have but absolutely." She looked up and asked, "Are you ready to have that conversation with your brother?"

"Everybody seems to think I should have had that conversation already, but it will be tough regardless," she admitted.

"And he might convince you to stay."

"Sure, but, like somebody just told me, that breakup is happening in six months anyway, and why would I want to push it to the end, when I'll feel more like I've been rousted out?" she mentioned, with a downturned lip.

"You've always been a mother hen to that brother of yours. You're what? Four years younger? Yet he's always just been your baby."

"And not necessarily in a good way," Giada admitted. "I think he needs six months alone, learning what independence looks like, before he gets married."

"Well, you've certainly been told that a few times. But we do understand that it's hard for you."

"It's something that I'll need to adjust to, possibly more than he will."

Dani gave her a commiserating smile. "You'll become an empty nester."

Giada laughed. "And I haven't even had a kid yet."

"No, but he's been that to you," she murmured, "and you've done a fantastic job."

"Wow. I have been a total mother hen to him, haven't I?" Giada shook her head. "It's just kind of sad."

"I get it. I really do. But I wouldn't worry about it as much as you are. He made the decision to get married. And six months from now, that'll be a completely different deal for him. And his fiancée needs to know what she's getting into too."

"I don't think he'll look at it that way, considering how much he'll suffer for six months."

"Is she a good cook?"

Giada looked at Dani in surprise. "You know what? I've never even asked. In our family, it's such a sexist thing, but the women are supposed to stay home to look after the men."

"Doesn't mean the new wife is of the same opinion," Dani noted, with a raised eyebrow. "Does the fiancée want to sit at home and wait for her dearly beloved to return?" she quipped, with a rolling eye look.

"I think not," Giada replied.

Dani shook her head. "I don't know that I would be happy at home, without work too. It's up to each individual. I know of an attorney, a woman, whose husband stays at home with their young daughter, does the cooking and cleaning. It works for all of them. Each doing what they enjoy. We all gotta be true to ourselves."

"In my family it was expected of me to keep looking after Francis. Obviously I got an education and worked at the same time. But, when I wouldn't bring home a husband right off the bat, following all the extended family's traditions," she teased, "I think they all thought that I was better off looking after Francis instead."

"Good Lord, treating you like the spinster sister already? You're only twenty-six," she stated. "How long has this been going on? At what point in time were you supposed to get married?"

"They'd have been happy to see me engaged at sixteen and wed when I turned eighteen, I think. Admittedly I wasn't really feeling it at that age."

"I would think not. How do you even know who you are and what you want while just a teen? You have to know yourself really well so you can choose your mate wisely."

"Agreed. Yet, now, with our parents gone," she stated, with a sad smile, "I won't have my father to walk me down the aisle."

Instantly Dani got up, walked around, and gave her a hug. "I know it still hurts," she said. "Sometimes those hurts just stay with us forever."

"And that's hardly fair, is it?" she asked, shaking off the blues and giving her boss a brighter smile. "At least my brother will get married, and that should make our parents happy, as they smile down from above."

"It will," Dani agreed, with a bright smile of her own. "You know it will. And what about you? Will you stay until he's married or not?"

"No." Giada shook her head. "I think he would be a better husband and a better partner if he does survive the next few months on his own."

"That doesn't mean he'll agree with you though," Dani warned her.

"I know. It's a discussion I need to have with him. But I wasn't sure if I had another place to go to. Hence me being here in your office."

"I'll get back to you to confirm," she stated, "but, if there isn't one right now, there will be soon."

"Well, *soon* would be something," Giada agreed, "even if I moved out in a month or two."

"Sure, but the sooner the better, probably."

"At least for my sake, maybe, yes." And, with that, she headed to her office. It would be a long day now, as she had done something that she'd been wondering about but had held back taking the plunge on because it would be uncomfortable for her and her brother. Yet what everybody had said here was right. It would hurt and would probably hurt her more than her brother. He'd be inconvenienced, but he had a fiancée now. Somebody he absolutely loved and adored. And that relationship would hopefully make him mature as well. And, for that to happen, for him to realize his own maximum potential, Giada needed to get out of the way. She groaned, as she sat back at her desk. "Why didn't I see that before now?"

And, because she hadn't seen it, it was hard to accept that she had been so focused on looking after him that she hadn't looked after his emotional needs and what was best for him in other ways too. Giada hadn't been looking after her own emotional needs and doing what was best for her either. *Huh.*

Trying to park her mental roller coaster, she set about getting through the rest of her day. She would talk to Francis tonight when she got home. They would have this discussion, and hopefully he wouldn't be too upset about it.

But, by the time she got home, and they sat down to a meal, he was already in an ugly mood, yet she persevered.

"You want to move out?" He stared at her in shock. "Why would you do that?"

"It would save me the trip back and forth," she explained, "and I think it's time you lived alone, before you got married."

"Well, that would be stupid," he said, with a dismissive wave of his hand. "I won't be alone very soon. Margaret will be moving in, so obviously I don't need that experience."

And he completely ignored the fact that it was something that *she* wanted to do and something that *he* needed to do. "I don't think so."

He waved his hand again in her face. "Stop. You're not moving out. What kind of a brother would I be? I fully expect you to stay on after we're married too. It's not like Margaret will know how to cook or anything right away."

Giada stared at him. Her heart sank. And then her anger burst free. "Did you just say that you expect me to stay on, *as your cook*, after you're married?"

"Yes, that's why we had a fight last week," he replied, with the shrug. "She didn't want that. Not that she doesn't like you of course," he added, with yet another airy dismissive hand wave.

Why had she not noticed all those hand movements all

this time? "I would agree with Margaret," Giada replied. "She's a new bride and expects to have the house to herself. Why would you even put that on her?"

He stared at her in surprise. "You know our families are always big and extended. If Mama were here, she would be staying in the house too."

At that, she stared at him in shock. "And that would be even harder on your bride."

"And she would adjust," he stated in a cool manner.

A manner so very much like her father that Giada could only stare. "I had never considered that you were so much like Papa," she noted quietly. She knew this conversation would likely be difficult, but it had never occurred to her that he expected her to stay on. And how Margaret didn't cook, so Giada was expected to stay on in that role too? "Besides," she added, "I need a life of my own."

"Well, you won't get it working in that place full of broken-down men," he replied in disgust. "I mean, you might as well stay here and look after us. At least then you might find a relationship through us."

"I'm not staying here and looking after you and your bride too," she stated firmly. "I'm not a spinster. I'm not an old maid. I'm not too old to have a family of my own or a relationship of my own," she argued, feeling her own temper spike yet again. "And I sure as heck am not staying here to look after the house."

"But you have to," he stated matter-of-factly. "It's the only way that Margaret would agree for you to stay."

"I'm not staying," she declared flatly. "So you guys can do your own dishes and your own vacuuming. Not to mention the cooking."

"Well, no," he replied simply. "I'd just hire somebody.

Why would anyone want to do that themselves?"

"But you're okay for me to do it?" she asked, getting angrier and angrier.

He shrugged, as if to say, *What's the problem here?*

Why had she not seen that before? Why had she allowed herself to be treated this way? Because she'd done what she'd done out of love, whereas he didn't appear to have any respect at all for her. "You think I'll just stay here after you're married and continue to look after you?"

He stared at her, bewildered. "Why would you not want to?"

Her jaw dropped. Slowly she closed it, looked down at her plate, realizing that absolutely everything had tasted like sawdust for at least the last ten minutes. Then she said quietly, "I'll head up to my room."

"Good," he replied, with feeling. "Hopefully by the time you come back down again you'll be back to normal."

"*Geesh.*" She shoved away her plate, stood, left the kitchen as it was, and went straight to her room. She sent a text to Dani. **The sooner, the better.**

Giada didn't expect any response right away, but Dani sent a text. **Tomorrow. There's a place for you. Come with your gear and stay.**

Giada pondered Dani's text for a long moment, and then she looked around at her place—her place—where she had lived all her life and realized that presented yet another problem. She didn't own any furniture. This was the family home, and Francis planned to stay in it. Indeed, he'd inherited it. She, on the other hand, had inherited a small amount of money, a dowry as some would probably look at it. But she didn't have anything really big to move. Yet at the same time, a lot of mementos, books, photos were here that she wasn't sure she wanted to just leave behind, risking them being tossed like trash.

Torn, and in a quandary as to how to proceed, she didn't answer Dani right away but headed to bed, confused, tired, emotionally overwrought. And hurt by her brother's words. The fact that he didn't even understand in what way he might have upset her hurt even more. Finally, exhausted, she closed her eyes and slept.

PERCY WOULD LIKE to say that he didn't notice Giada's absence for the next couple days, but he had to admit that, every time he turned around, he half expected to see her.

Finally Shane interrupted one of their sessions and said, "She's not here. Stop looking for her."

He stared at him in shock. "What?"

"I can see you," Shane stated. "You're not giving 100 percent because you keep looking at the doorway, hoping that Giada will pop in."

He flushed. "I just … I haven't seen her for a while." He frowned. "Is she okay?"

"She's having some home issues," Shane noted. "She's working at getting it resolved now."

He leaned forward immediately. "But she's okay, right? Her brother isn't stopping her?"

"I don't think so," Shane replied, looking at him in surprise.

"I know that we were talking about how potentially she would move here, but she told me that it would be a very hard conversation for her brother."

"I don't think he'd do anything to physically harm her

though," Shane stated. And then he stopped, looked at Percy, and added, "Unless you know something I don't know."

"I don't know very much at all." Percy raised both hands, feeling his body wrench with the movement. He hissed at the pain and slowly laid back down again, waiting for the ripples to shudder through him.

"Well, I'll tell you what. If it'll make you focus better, I'll get Dani to check up on her."

"That would be great." Percy waited while Shane booked it down the hallway. Percy heard the sound of Shane running, and Percy was jealous to hear that sound of power and control, something he was striving for and one day hoped to get back. Something he *needed* to get back.

Just that sense of being in control of your body and not having things flop when you didn't want things to flop and not having things flip when you didn't want them to flip. He shook his head at that. He carefully went through the exercises Shane had given him because Shane wasn't here in case Percy ran into trouble. By the time he finished the next set, Shane was back again. "Well? Is she okay?"

He grinned. "She's taken a couple days off."

"Really? She didn't say anything about that."

"No, maybe not, but Dani said that she'll move into an apartment over here pretty quickly, so that's probably why."

"Oh," Percy said in delight. "Good for her. I guess that means everything went okay with the brother."

"Well, Dani got a text this morning, saying Giada wouldn't be in, but I don't know that anybody's heard about how the conversation with the brother went."

He nodded but felt an odd sense of disquiet. "I don't feel very good about that," he replied in a low tone.

Shane settled back on his heels. "What do you mean?"

"I don't think that brother of hers will be very happy at all that she's leaving."

"Are you thinking that he'll do something stupid?"

"I would hope not," Percy murmured. "That would be pushing things too far. But I don't think it'll be quite so easy to leave as she's thinking."

Shane nodded quietly. "Well, lots of people are here she can call on to help, if it becomes ugly."

"True." After he did another set, gasping and lying on his back on the floor, his mind was once again consumed with thoughts of her and what she had ahead of her. He asked Shane, "Would she even tell you guys?"

"I don't know," Shane admitted, "I might talk to Dani after your session."

"That sounds like a good idea. I don't have her phone number, so I can't call to see if she's okay. And that's not exactly a smart thing to do in this instance, I'm sure. I'm just a patient here," he noted. "Yet we kind of hit it off, but that's all."

"Don't knock yourself that way," Shane stated. "She's been good for you, and you've been good for her. After your talks, that seemed to be the added impetus for her leaving, I'm sure."

He wasn't so sure about that. "I hate to see people take advantage of others, and it seemed like that brother was pushing things to the limit."

"Well, I've seen him once, and he's one of those sulky types, who thinks the world owes him."

Percy winced at that. "And he's the one getting married? Makes you wonder, doesn't it?"

"Right? But, as long as they're happy, what we think

doesn't matter."

"No, I know, and it's one thing to stress over some things, but it's another thing to over stress."

At that, Shane laughed. "And it's one thing to use a discussion like this to get out of your work. What we can't do is let discussions of her overtake our work today."

"I'm working. I'm working," Percy stated. "Besides, we're still experimenting to see what we can do and what we can't do."

At that, Shane burst out laughing.

Percy grinned at him. "See? I'm not always working the angles."

"People *always* work the angles," Shane declared. "You're talking about her brother working angles? It's human nature. Everybody's trying to figure out how to get the best deal for themselves."

"Wow, you guys must see a lot of humanity, don't you?" Percy muttered. And he did another set of exercises, feeling the sweat break out all over his body. When he collapsed back down from this one, he groaned.

"And now you're done," Shane stated.

"Oh, thank God," he muttered. "I didn't think I could do that last one."

"You can always do more than you think," Shane noted. "But, in this case, I don't want you doing more than you think you can do because, right now, like you said, we're still testing, still exploring the limits of what your body can do, before we ask it to push past that point. So there's life after this, and we have to make sure that you don't end up in pain again."

"And how will we prevent that?" he asked. "Because I can already feel it coming on." And then he cried out, his body twitching to the left with muscle cramps.

"No, no, no," Shane said immediately, as he shifted Percy to his side. "Just relax. I'll do some work on the back here." And he quickly worked the insertion points on the muscles.

Percy shuddered as the pain kicked in again and then again. By the time the seizing stopped, he collapsed on his stomach on the floor. He was exhausted. "I really need that to stop."

"Slowly you'll notice that there'll be a distance between sessions and those cramps, and that will widen as you get better and stronger," Shane explained.

"Maybe," he replied, rolling over on his back, slowly gasping in agony. "They just wipe me right out."

"Do you want to try the hot tub again?"

"Yeah, I really do. But it's morning. Is that okay?"

"It's about ten-thirty," Shane noted, "and that's totally fine, as long as you're up for it."

"I want to be up for it," he admitted. "It felt a lot better in the morning, and I even slept beautifully last night."

"Good, let's get you into the chair." And Shane helped Percy up and over to the wheelchair. "Now we'll go to your room, get you changed and down there." It took a bit, but, by the time they finally reached the pool area, Shane asked, "Hot tub or pool?"

"Hot tub for the muscles," he said instantly.

Shane looked over at Percy. "You a swimmer? Do you want to try the pool first? Then the hot tub?"

"Sure, let's try the pool first," Percy agreed.

And, with that, Shane shifted the angle of the wheelchair, brought him over to the pool, and locked the wheels, so that he could stand up and then hold on to the pool railing. Shane watched as Percy placed his remaining foot along the edge of the pool, and, using the railing, pulled himself up from his wheelchair by himself. Rather than a graceful dive into the pool, Percy literally flung himself into the water and sank right to the bottom. And then he bounced right back up to the top, broke through the surface, with a cry of joy.

"Now this is more like it." Shane laughed. "I gather this makes it all worthwhile?"

"If this is the reward every day," Percy replied, "you will have no problem getting me to work like a madman. The water is where I belong."

And, with that, he dove back under yet again.

Chapter 9

G IADA WALKED INTO work the following morning and got busy. Taking a couple of days off was one thing but showing up late two days in a row? Well, that wouldn't be good. And yet she was still tired, stressed, and emotionally overwrought. To say that the discussion with her brother hadn't gone well was an understatement. And he had doubled down on his stance, letting her know in no uncertain terms that absolutely no way would she be allowed to leave.

She hadn't even considered that he would put up this kind of a fight. She was her own person, had been for a very long time—almost a decade. Yes, she and her brother had had many family members there for them in Giada's and Francis's early childhood and teenage years, and they all had been very close during that time. However, since then, Giada and Francis had lost both sets of grandparents and their own parents. So what remained of their big Italian family was now more remote relatives, like second cousins twice removed and the like, many still living in Italy.

So she wasn't at all sure that some emotional attachment to her or their extended family was causing him so much stress, as much as it could have just been the fact that she was leaving. That change was happening. She was better at change than he was, but still they both suffered with the consequences. And, in this case, it was big change all-around. She had come to terms with the fact that he was getting married and that Giada's childhood home would no longer be her home. She had just recently made her decision as to what she would do about it.

More freedom was ahead of her. She wouldn't lie; she'd been looking forward to it. That kind of freedom she could get behind. Francis was making major changes and bringing a partner into his life, and that was great for him. But it wouldn't do Giada any good if she still lived there. Being the third wheel was the last thing she wanted to do, or, even worse, an unpaid housekeeper and cook for Francis *and* Margaret. Her brother had even started making noise about stopping her from going to work. She had never even heard him talk like that before.

Yet her father had caused quite a kerfuffle when her mother had wanted to work. But her mother had backed down, preferring to stay home, after her husband had explained what the workforce was like. Giada had often wondered at her mother's choice, but, as her mother was very much a homemaker, Giada hadn't really questioned it. And nobody had questioned Giada's decision to get out and have a career, especially when it was obvious that she wasn't looking to get married anytime soon.

Times had changed since that previous generation, and maybe that was the blessing Giada hadn't even been aware of that she had been granted. Nothing like finding out the world around you had not changed in one fell swoop.

The house was legally her brother's, and she hadn't felt bad staying there all this time, but no way did she want to stay there now. And it was strange because, of course, her mother had done the same thing. Once married, she'd moved into a house already occupied by her own mother-in-law and father-in-law. However, as soon as the newlyweds could afford it, Giada's parents had moved into their own place—the home Giada and Francis grew up in. But, in this case, the story was different because, of course, this was her brother's place.

Confused, upset, Giada buried herself in her work all day. When she finally lifted her head and realized she was almost in danger of missing out on lunch, she quickly got to her feet and strode down the hallway. The dining area was quiet, which said a lot about the time of day. As she walked in, she saw Dennis vacuuming the room. She winced. "I guess no food is left?" she asked, looking over at the coffee to see if something along the lines of a sandwich were in the nearby coolers.

"There are leftovers," he replied, walking over, studying her face. "Are you okay?"

She frowned but nodded. "Yeah, but taking off yesterday caused a backlog of work, and I've been buried since I got back."

"What can I get you?" he asked, as he moved behind the counter.

"How about some leftovers from lunch, maybe reheated?" she asked hopefully. "I didn't get breakfast either."

At that, his eyebrows shot up. "I can make you something fresh, like an omelet, but we do have some leftover chicken, and I think even some fajitas."

"Both would be good," she noted. "Any veggies?"

"Let me make you a plate. Missing breakfast is one thing. Missing breakfast and lunch?" He shook his head. "That's not cool."

"No, but it happens," she admitted, "more often than

I'd like to think."

He nodded and then headed into the back area. She wandered around, looking at the coffee, and decided the last thing she needed was yet more caffeine. She did pick up a couple cookies for dessert and grabbed a bottle of juice. Maybe also not the best choice because of the carbs in each. Would likely send her blood sugar right up and drop it again. But, hey, some choices she had to accommodate.

When Dennis returned with an overflowing tray of food, she stared in astonishment. "Just because I didn't eat earlier today doesn't mean there's room to stuff in all that now." But she laughed when she looked at it. "Wow, I won't need dinner tonight after this."

Almost instantly her mind was grateful for that because she could avoid going home anytime soon. She smiled at Dennis. "Thank you."

She added the bottle of juice and the cookies to the tray, carefully making her way with it back in her office. She wanted to shut her office door to close out the world, but it wasn't to be. She was still plowing through her lunch, when a knock came at her open door, and she looked up to see Dani standing there.

"Hey," Dani greeted her. "How was your time off?"

"Horrible," she replied bluntly.

At that, Dani's eyebrows popped up. "You had a few people worried about you."

"Why's that?" she asked, frowning.

"Well, for one, Percy had a terrible feeling that you weren't okay, and he sent Shane down to check that all was well with you. And when I told Shane that you had the day off, that seemed to make Percy even more fretful."

She stared at her boss and friend in surprise, slowly lowering the fork. "Oh my." She frowned. "Did Percy have a particular concern?"

Dani nodded slowly, leaned against the doorjamb, and crossed her arms over her chest. "Percy didn't feel good about your brother letting you go and was afraid that he would do something stupid."

Giada almost felt sick to her stomach, as she realized just how accurate Percy's assessment was. "I hate to say it," she noted, "but Percy was more right than wrong."

Dani walked in, sat down in the spare chair, and said, "Maybe you should tell me more about this."

Giada nodded and explained what went on.

Dani immediately frowned and shook her head. "I get that now, with his change and yours, he'll assert his *head of the household* mind-set and probably be even more insufferable," Dani replied, with an eye roll, "but that's quite a feudal mentality."

"And not one I expected," she admitted quietly. "I don't know how come, all of a sudden, he's feeling this way, but I suspect it's insecurity."

"And how. In a big way. … Yet what does he have to feel insecure about?" Dani asked, looking at her in surprise.

"Change," she replied bluntly. "My brother doesn't handle it well."

"Well, he's the one getting married."

"I hate to say it, but there's a good chance that, even if I caused a stink about it, he might prefer to break that off in order to avoid another major disruption. If I were to still live in the house, then he would only have to deal with the addition of living with someone, sharing the house and his bedroom with his soon-to-be wife. But the addition of Margaret, plus the loss of me, not to mention the change in circumstances with the control and management of the household, and all that comes with that, namely cooking and cleaning," she noted quietly, "is possibly too much for him."

Dani stared at her in surprise.

Giada shrugged. "I know. It's. … It sounds foolish. I get it. But sometimes we find certain behaviors very difficult to control, and he and I, both of us, don't handle change well," she admitted. "But we didn't have to deal with it, until something major happened."

"Of course," Dani agreed. "But it hadn't occurred to me that he would be …" And she hesitated, at a loss for words.

"Don't get me wrong. He wasn't violent," she clarified. "He didn't …" She stopped because she was about to say, *He didn't threaten me*—yet actually he did. "I don't think his threats had merit. Let me put it that way."

"But he *did* threaten you?" Dani asked, horror on her face.

"I was trying to work my way through that just now," Giada replied. "The answer is yes and no. I think it was an implied threat, which could be construed as a threat, yes. I don't want to think of it as a threat, so I'll say, *No, it wasn't a threat.*" And then she burst out laughing. "You can clearly see that we can't handle some things in life, so we shift the blame to make the change look not quite so unpleasant—in this case, the change of the beliefs and the behaviors of my brother."

"I get all that psychobabble," Dani stated bluntly. "But the bottom line is, are you in danger?"

It made Giada sick to her stomach that somebody would even have to ask that question. She slowly put down her fork, staring at the fabulous food she'd been eating. "I don't think so."

"Because, if that is a problem, you know I can send somebody to collect your stuff."

"And you know what? As I was looking around my place, I don't even own very much," she explained. "It's been my home since childhood. In case you hadn't heard, it's … it's our family home. Then, with both my parents gone, of course, my brother inherited everything."

"But your parents had *two* children. He's the eldest." At that, Dani winced. "So he inherits everything, including all the furniture, and you just have personal belongings, correct?"

Giada smiled and nodded. "Yes. Don't … don't get me wrong, I did inherit as well. Nothing quite so much as my brother got, but, of course, that's also very much a cultural thing," she noted. "My brother is supposed to be the head of the household now and to make decisions that the head of the household would normally make," she explained. "Yes, my family was very backward in that way."

"Very," Dani agreed. "I do have an apartment for you. It is ready. It still needs a cleaning yet. However, if you want it, it's yours."

At that, Giada's jaw dropped. "So I can move in before it's cleaned?"

Dani nodded. "Yes, and there's absolutely no reason not to, especially if you are in any way uncomfortable about the situation at home."

"I …" She stopped. "I really don't know about the situation at home," she admitted. "I don't want to even think that that would be a problem, and he wasn't violent, but I also don't want to go home." She faced Dani. "I have never felt so horrible in my own home. And I don't want to see that threatening part of him rise to the surface."

"Was your father ever abusive?"

"No, he loved my mother to distraction, but he did have a temper on him. The only things that would really spike that temper were things like her getting a job. She wanted a job. She wanted to go out and do something. He thought it was all about money and didn't understand that it was to feel useful. To him, she could be doing all that useful stuff by looking after him. He didn't seem to understand my mother's need for independence. And, of course, in his patriarchal world, he didn't want her to have independence because, well"—she shrugged—"because honestly he wanted her dependent on him."

"But that's about power and control, not love," Dani stated in a low tone.

"And I hadn't really looked at it that way before." She tapped her finger on her desktop. "Let me talk to Francis again. And, if it ends up being a problem, I guess then I'll take you up on your offer for some assistance." Dani obviously didn't like that answer. "He won't beat me up, and he won't lock me inside," she stated with some determination, yet frowned. "I guess, if I don't show up tomorrow and if I don't contact you, then maybe you'll take this conversation into consideration." She looked down at her food again. "Will I really get to eat here all the time?"

Dani laughed. And the sound was a relief for both of them. "Absolutely."

SHANE WALKED IN, with a bright smile. "Now you don't have to worry anymore," he told Percy. "Giada is at work this morning."

For Percy, it was such a relief. "I'm really glad to hear that. I've never been the kind of person to have terrible premonitions, but instincts have always been something I've honored," he explained. "Kept me alive in many uncomfortable situations. And that whole scenario with her brother just feels very wrong. Still does."

"And I never even thought about it," Shane admitted, "until you brought it up. Her family is from a very old Sicilian line. And, since the father died, the son has taken over the reins of the household."

"In theory. And yet," Percy added, "not the actual running of the house itself."

"Well, he would see that as women's work, wouldn't he?" Shane asked.

"In that case, who'll look after him now that Giada's leaving?"

"Hearing more about that family background, it's also quite possible that her brother never expected Giada to move, even after he married."

"And what? Just keep her as some unpaid housekeeper and cook?"

"Don't forget that unmarried daughters would often look after the household for their siblings," Shane noted.

"Yeah, one hundred years ago," Percy cried out.

Shane laughed. "Sure, but the brother's been a little unchecked in these past few years, so it's hard to say how he'll handle anybody going against him."

"See? That's why it's important to shake things up sometimes," Percy replied, as he made his way onto the mat for Shane's first set of workups. "You don't get so stuck in your ways, where you think that your word is law."

"Well, she seems fine. I just saw her getting a late

lunch."

"Ah, maybe she got in late today."

"No, I think she's been stuck in her office, trying to make up for being gone."

"Makes sense too." By the time Percy completed his workout, he felt pretty exhausted.

Shane asked, "So do you want to try for the pool again?"

"I want to try," Percy replied, "because I know the reward is worth it. Yet today it feels a very long way away."

"So we just won't then," Shane offered. "Time for a shower, even a rest before dinner."

Percy had to admit that maybe Shane was right. He nodded slowly. "I really hate to, but I think I might have to."

"Good enough," Shane agreed. "I'll see you tomorrow." He waited at the doorway to make sure that Percy could make his own way back into his wheelchair. Shane nodded at the stump and asked, "Still no progress on a prosthetic?"

"No. They did tell me that it would likely be three to four to even five months."

Shane nodded again. "I'll make a note of it." And, with that, he was gone.

Slowly making his way to his room, Percy felt an exhaustion taking over his muscles that he hadn't felt in a very long time. The pool would have been a good idea; the hot tub probably would have been a better idea. But he really didn't have the energy to get there. Depressed over that, plus hating the fact that he wasn't quite mobile yet, he reached his room and managed to get into a hot shower. That helped a lot.

But today was just an off day, a day of struggling to even feel normal. He would put that down to the fact that he had been worried about Giada all yesterday and last night. And she was here today and apparently doing much better, so

Percy was good with that. After the shower, he dressed, thought about a snack, and then gave up that notion, crashed on the bed, and fell asleep for a nap. He woke to the sound of somebody gasping.

"Oh, I'm sorry. I didn't mean to disturb you."

He recognized her voice and called out, "Wait." He slowly and warily rolled to his back—in case the muscles started to spasm again. That accomplished, he saw Giada staring at him in concern. "I'm fine," he replied, giving her the briefest of smiles.

"Well, don't call me a liar," she stated, "but you sure don't look fine."

"No, I'm sure I don't. It was a hard session with Shane today. We're down to the brass tacks of what I really need to be doing, and there's nothing easy or nice about any of those rehab exercises," he admitted.

"I'm sorry," she said gently. "That sounds terrible."

He waved a hand, as if to brush away her concerns. "How was your time off?" he asked quietly. "I was going to text you and wish you well but realized I didn't have your number.

"It was … okay." She walked closer to him pulling out her phone and said, "Give me your number."

He did and his phone buzzed with a text from her. A big happy face. He grinned. "Thanks." He put his phone down. "And your brother? How's he doing."

"Well, my brother's struggling," she admitted. "I've spoken to Dani, and there is a place here for me. I could move in today, if I wanted to. I'll talk to my brother, see if he could give me a hand. Otherwise, I may need to accept Dani's offer to get someone to help me move."

"I'd accept Dani's offer anyway," Percy suggested, with a

smile. "Why wouldn't you?"

"Because maybe that's something my brother would like to do," she noted gently.

Percy frowned at that.

"My brother isn't an ogre. He's … just got some things to adjust to."

Right. In Percy's mind, that sounded exactly like the worn-out irrational excuses of a battered wife, heard by many over and over again. "I get it," he stated, looking at her. "Just make sure it doesn't become something worse."

She winced. "Everybody seems to have the same thought. It never occurred to me that anybody would have a reason to worry."

"How did he sound when you talked to him?"

"Angry," she admitted immediately. "He seemed to think that I would stay in the house, even after they were married."

He stared at her in surprise. "Is that what you want to do?"

"Heck no," she stated immediately. "I'm … looking forward to the personal freedom of living on my own. And honestly, I should have moved out a long time ago. Everyone was so right about that."

"Doesn't matter if others are right or not," he argued. "It's not those people's decision. It's not those people's emotions. It's yours. If you weren't quite ready before, then you weren't quite ready."

"Yeah, I wasn't quite ready," she agreed, "but not because I was lonely but because I knew he would not handle it well."

"So then maybe it was past time," Percy stated, with a head tilt. "And, of course, it will still be hard on you regardless."

"Yes," she noted, with a whimsical smile. "I love him. He's my brother, and we've been very close."

Percy nodded slowly. "I'm hearing a *but*."

"No *but*," she stated firmly. "I just think that he will be happier, once he's had a chance to adjust. That adjustment period will be rough though."

"But rough for him to handle that change," he reminded her. "That's not your job. You can't do it for him."

She laughed. "And that's a good thing. I got suckered into doing enough of his homework growing up."

"Seriously?"

"Yeah. There's only four years between us. Yet, when he hit college and had to write reports, I used to do them for him."

"Good Lord, why would you help him cheat?"

"I don't know," she muttered, staring at him in surprise. "I hadn't really considered it that way."

"What other way is there?"

"He would tell me that he didn't have the time or he wasn't feeling well, things like that," she explained. "So I didn't mind, and I would do it for him."

"You didn't mind, or you didn't even think about it?" he asked, staring at her.

"I don't know." She frowned. "I'm starting to see a lot of things in a different light."

"Good," he stated. "Sounds like you've been brainwashed and manipulated for a very long time."

"No," she argued, anger stirring in her tone. "That's not fair."

"If you say so, but you've already been doing everything he's asked of you. It just seems a shame that, at this point in time, you would have any argument at all about having your own life."

"And I don't know for sure that there is an argument," she said, looking around his room now. "I'm just checking to make sure you were okay."

"I'm fine." Percy didn't particularly appreciate that she felt she *had* to come check that he was okay. He would have hoped that she cared enough to. "I'm not doing too badly today. I'm just tired and needed a nap."

She nodded, frowning at him.

"Nope," he replied. "You don't get to worry about me like that."

"That's fine," she agreed a little too eagerly, "but then you don't get to worry about me like that either." And, with that gentle reprimand, she turned and walked away.

Chapter 10

W ITH EVERYBODY SO petrified about her brother's behavior, Giada found herself nervous on her way home. She'd never been nervous around her brother before. She didn't like it either. As she walked into the house, she heard no sounds. She walked up to her room and started sorting and packing, before cooking dinner. It would take some time to decide what to take with her and what to leave behind, and she didn't have much time tonight, but she would make good use of the time she had.

After she had gone through her closet, she was already pretty tired. She walked downstairs, checking the clock in the living room. She had seafood defrosting in the fridge since last night. She would sear a salmon fillet and cook some rice and toss a nice Caesar salad. As she walked into the kitchen, she started in surprise. "Hey," she said, seeing her brother there. "I didn't hear you in the house earlier."

He looked up at her and nodded. It looked like he'd been drinking. Instinctively she withdrew. "How was your day at work?" she asked him.

"It was fine," he replied in a harsh tone.

She winced. "My day was fine too. I was about to cook dinner. Are you ready to eat?"

"Of course I'm ready," he snapped. "We eat at the same time every day without fail. Why would it change today?"

She took a slow deep breath. "Hey, I just asked a question. I'm not sure what's going on but don't take your temper out on me."

"That works both ways," he replied. "You're the one taking your temper out on me."

She stared at him in surprise. "What are you talking about?"

"You're moving out," he stated angrily. "You didn't have to. You didn't have any reason to even look at that option," he argued. "If you didn't like Margaret, you could have told me."

"Of course I like Margaret," she replied. "What's that got to do with anything? She's beautiful. She's a wonderful person." If, in Giada's mind, she couldn't quite understand why Margaret wanted her brother, that was a different story. And likely only sour grapes on her part. "I don't know where that even came from," she explained, "but your fiancée's a beautiful person."

"Yes, but, if I'd realized you didn't think that she was appropriate for me, then I might have reconsidered."

"And that's not what I would want from you at all," she stated firmly, walking over to stand in front of him, squaring her shoulders. "Why would you even get that impression?"

"Why are you talking about moving out?" he asked bluntly.

"Because *I* want to," she stated with emphasis. "Because it's time. Because I want to have my own life."

He stared at her and shook his head. "You're not married. You don't have a man to look after you. You should remain at home. Papa would be furious."

"Papa lived like the family from generations ago," she noted. "Times have changed. You know perfectly well that his method of keeping us all compliant is no longer something that works today."

"Of course it does," he said, looming over her.

"No," she snapped, standing up to him. "That's nonsense. And I'm not letting you pull that over on me."

"I'm the head of this household."

"That's nice," she said. "But this household does not include having rights over my life. It's your house. I know that. It's always been your house. It was given to you, but that doesn't mean that you get to decide what I do with my life from here on in."

He glared at her. "So what now? You're jealous that I got the house? Of course it's my house," he snapped. "I'm the son."

And such arrogance filled his tone of voice that she stared at him in disbelief. "Did you just say that?" she asked, studying him. "Like where the heck is that coming from?"

He waved his hand. "It's the way it's always been done. That's the problem with you. You never found anybody to marry you, so you're part of my household then," he stated. "I never even had a chance to have a life without looking after you."

"Oh my." She huffed, taking a step back. "Did you really just say that?"

"Well, you've always been here. It's not like any boyfriends were around for you. It's not like you'll ever get married," he replied, his temper flaring. "Do you think that it was easy for me to get Margaret to agree that you would stay here? But she's a good Italian woman, and she understands, although it wasn't easy," he admitted. "I have a responsibility to look after you," he stated, completely turning the tables on how she had been thinking.

"So you think," she said, "that you're responsible for me and that you have to look after me?" She shook her head. "Good Lord. Maybe we're more of a mess than I thought," she muttered.

He frowned. "What are you talking about?"

"You don't have to look after me," she stated. "I have a career. I have a job. I'm perfectly fine to look after myself."

"Yes, but you're alone," he noted. "It's ... it's not like you'll ever have money to buy your own house, not like the money I have. That's why I was given more from our parents, as they knew I would be responsible for your care. So I have to look after you," he explained, "until you have your own home, until you have a husband."

"I'm not asking for your permission to leave and to move out and to live on my own. So don't expect me to ask for your permission regarding any future husband of mine—or any decisions regarding my life."

"You see? That's the problem with you getting an education," he stated, standing with his hands on his hips. "You know Papa didn't want you to."

"I know Papa didn't want a lot of things," she replied coolly, trying to restrain her own temper because this was not the time to lose it. It would just prove that she was not quite ready and mature enough to handle this. It was so frustrating to hear him talk like this, like she had no value outside of being a baby-making machine. She shook her head. "Does Margaret understand how you view women?"

"You leave her out of this," he said hotly.

"Yeah, well, that would be nice if I could, but you're the one who brought it up, saying that you had to really convince her to let me stay here."

"She's a beautiful person with a good heart," he replied.

"She saw reason eventually."

Giada winced at that. "It's normal for her to want to have the house to yourselves to start your married life out with just the two of you, on your own," she explained to her brother. "I'm surprised you would even try to convince her of anything different."

"What's important is that she understands her duty," he snapped.

"Whoa, whoa, whoa, whoa, whoa, whoa!" She stared at him. "I sure hope you didn't present it in that light."

"Why not?" he asked, throwing his head back and glaring at her.

"Because there's a lot more to Margaret than just being your dutiful wife. Or have you forgotten that she's in school right now? And that she's planning on having her own business?"

"But that's only until she has babies," he stated. "And then she'll stay home with them."

"She'll stay home with them," Giada said in outrage, "only if *she* wants to."

"No, she won't have a choice."

"Wow. I wonder if she really does understand what marriage to you means." On the inside, Giada couldn't help but wonder if she needed to talk with Margaret herself. Giada would hate to see her brother left all alone, but she would hate to imagine Margaret—as a beautiful free spirit but very gentle—suffering at the hands of her brother's ancient, archaic beliefs that the little woman belonged at home where she could look after her spouse.

"You forget about her," he snapped. "I will look after her."

"Yeah, you will stifle her, and you'll crush her spirit and

put her into an early grave, so that she becomes nothing more than Mama was."

"Don't you insult our mama like that," he roared.

"I'm not insulting her at all, but I am certainly not underestimating the fact that Mama wanted more out of life, that she wanted to do something other than just look after Papa."

"If she wanted that, she could have that," he replied.

"Really? Papa wouldn't have let her have a job," she snapped. "And you know that."

"Because it was for her own good," he snarled.

She stared at him. "I don't even feel like I know you anymore," she stated in bewilderment.

"Of course you do," he retorted. "I'm the same as I always have been."

"If that's the case," she noted sadly, "I haven't seen you clearly for a *very* long time." And, on that note, she turned and headed to her bedroom, where she threw herself down on the bed and, dry-eyed, stared at the ceiling, wondering what had just happened.

GIADA'S LAST WORDS had stuck in Percy's head for the rest of the day and night and still floated in his mind when he woke the next morning. If she wasn't allowed to worry about him, then he wasn't allowed to worry about her. Was that fair? Of course in some ways it was, but their situations were completely different. But, in essence, the theme shared between them was the same.

They cared.

And when you care, you worry.

He trusted her to handle her brother, but Percy also knew her brother had some issues. Although her brother *might* be in control, that didn't mean he wouldn't lose control. And some family dynamics were harder to break free from than others.

Shane poked his head through the open doorway. "We're meeting in ten, but we'll be in the water for the next hour. So, instead of heading to the workout room, I'll meet you downstairs instead. See you there." And, with that, he was gone.

Of all the changes Shane could have made to Percy's schedule, the pool was the best one yet. It took him a few minutes to get ready, to grab a towel and a T-shirt for the sun afterward to protect his skin, depending on Shane's plans afterward. Percy slowly made his way to the pool area.

There, without waiting, he locked the wheels to his wheelchair at the edge of the pool, stood on his good foot, dropped the items he'd been carrying on the chair, and fell over the side to crash into the cool refreshing water below.

Was there anything better?

Chapter 11

WHEN GIADA WALKED in that morning, Dani stood there in the lobby, staring at Giada in concern. She smiled. "Yeah, it's still difficult," she confirmed. "I'm working my way through the stuff that I own. He's not happy, but we're getting there."

With relief on her face, Dani smiled. "Good, but remember the offer to get you some moving help still stands. We should have your apartment all clean and ready for you in a couple days. But you can move in this very moment if need be. The housekeepers can work around your stuff, no problem. We also have some extra furniture if you need anything. Some of our units are furnished but over time people buy stuff they want for themselves and we store the extra until needed."

"And all that would be good," she stated. "It feels like I need to get out as soon as possible." She shrugged. "It'll just extend the pain to stay."

"Sorry, sweetheart." Dani gave her a big hug and then headed off to her office.

Following suit, Giada sat down in her desk chair, realizing that, with all the changes and disruptions going on at home and at work, she hadn't necessarily caught up with Percy and what was going on in his life. She hadn't meant to ignore him. And things might have ended on a little tense moment when they last spoke. When things kind of blew up at home and at work, she'd been keeping to herself out of privacy for her own sake. But it was definitely past time to check in on Percy.

Starting with that thought, she passed his room. The door was open, but nobody was there. She frowned at that and kept on walking. As she got to the dining area, she looked around the room and then outside, finding him seated on the deck. She grabbed a coffee and walked forward to join him, clearing her throat gently so as not to surprise him. When he turned and looked at her, she saw a warm greeting on his face. It made her feel immeasurably better. "Hey, I really don't have time to stop and sit, but I'm glad to see you."

"I'm glad to see you too," he replied. "Are you okay?"

She nodded. "My brother's not terribly happy about my decision, but he's accepting it." At least she hoped he would.

"At least you're hoping so," he noted cautiously.

She smiled. "And that's just what I was thinking. I might contact his fiancée today and have a talk with her."

He frowned and then shrugged. "You'll have to do the best that you can do for you," he noted. "I don't know the situation. Can't say I've ever been in it. I just know that sometimes guys don't take kindly to being told they can't have something."

She laughed. "I think that's all guys," she noted. "And it's not just guys either. Women are often the same too."

He grinned. "Well, I'm glad it's not the trauma that you thought it was."

She shrugged. "It's all good. Hopefully in a few days I'll have moved here anyway."

"And that would be lovely," he agreed. "I'm happy to see

you more often."

She smiled, feeling pleasure whisper through her. "And that feeling is mutual. So give me a chance to get moved in, and then we'll see what we can set up." With that, she raced back to her office. Nothing quite like knowing that you were wanted to make you feel like a whole new person. And Percy had definitely managed to make her feel wanted.

THE NEXT FEW days went by in a whirlwind, where she raced home, packed for an hour or so, made dinner, and left it for him with a note, before heading back to her room with her own meal, trying to get through as much of the cleaning and sorting and packing as she needed to.

It was an emotional time because, as she sorted through all the boxes of memorabilia, she also had to deal with the typical stuff saved by her parents—Giada's and Francis's childhood artwork that had covered the refrigerator for a time, those handmade Christmas ornaments, kindergarten graduation certificates, report cards, even a well-done term paper or two, with an A+ grade earned. So much stuff was left that her parents had saved. And Giada had never cleaned any of that out either. It was like she was processing their deaths by going through all this, saved from decades ago.

SHE HAD SLEPT the night before, yet she felt so drained that next day at work. She figured it was more about emotions than anything physical. After closing a set of files, her phone rang. "Hey, Margaret. What's up?"

"I'm calling to ask you that," she replied. "Are you okay?"

"I'm okay," Giada stated, but she didn't elaborate.

Margaret hesitated. "Your brother seems to think that you don't feel like you're welcome at the house."

An awkward silence followed. Giada shook her head. Her brother was not listening to her.

"You know I never wanted that, … never wanted you to feel that way," Margaret rushed to say.

"I had no intention of staying once he was married anyway," she stated, with a smile. "And thanks for being worried about me, but I'm fine."

"I know he really wants you to stay."

"He wants me to stay, but I'm not sure he wants me to stay for the right reason," she replied quietly. "He's even made a bunch of threats about it."

Margaret gasped. "I'm kind of worried about it because he's so adamant that you should stay."

"But is he adamant that I should stay because he cares about me," Giada asked quietly, "or adamant I should stay because he hasn't approved of me leaving?"

At that, Margaret whispered, "I don't know. It does make me rethink my own position."

"As much as I love my brother, I think you should. Take it seriously. Maybe have a talk with him about it," Giada suggested, "because, as you know, he … he's not the easiest person. And he's taken on an awful lot of our father's archaic characteristics just recently," she stated in bewilderment. "I don't even know what brought it on."

"Well, what brought it on," Margaret stated, "was you decided you would leave."

"But he's getting married, and, of course, you'll want the

house to yourself," she said in frustration. "How can he possibly think that he or you would want me to stay?"

"I don't know, and I … believe me. I'm not trying to kick you out. I know that you two have been close."

"We have been," she agreed, "but this discussion has done a lot to break us up. I love my brother, but, man, I don't want to live with him forever," she stated. "Neither do I have any intention of being the cook or taking over the laundry and cleaning like a maid, once you two get married," she cried out.

"Oh, my God," Margaret said. "And I'm worried about that too."

"He needs to be alone before you ever marry him," Giada suggested. "He's completely useless. So he has no idea what is involved in taking care of himself, much less the house, and doesn't appreciate all I've done. Won't appreciate all you do either at this rate."

"I know. I know. I was worried about that too. But he told me not to worry about it and that I won't have to do it all because that's one very big house."

"And that's true. I guess both of you could … afford to bring in a cleaning lady."

"Yeah," she agreed. "I just … I'm not honestly sure that that's what he was thinking about."

And such reluctance was in Margaret's tone that Giada stopped, winced, and said, "Yeah, he was thinking of me as the cleaning lady again, wasn't he? I think he's trying to bring back the family life from generations ago," she said, rushing to her brother's defense. "I can certainly see him trying to do that because that's how Papa did things, and Francis would probably consider himself a failure if he doesn't get the family unit solid," she murmured. "But that's not his job to do for me. I'll have my own family someday. Except Francis doesn't believe it, right? He thinks that I'm an old maid, even though I'm not very old."

"I know, and I'm sorry because it's so frustrating, and it seems like there's absolutely nothing I can do to clarify in his head that that's just not right."

"No, he's got it stuck in his head that that's the only way it is," she stated quietly. "I am cleaning up, cleaning out, and getting rid of a lot of my parents' stuff from my childhood and later school years, so that I can move," she explained, "and it will be a lot easier on me to not have to look after Francis anymore."

"I'm sorry," Margaret said. "It makes me feel terrible to think that this is happening."

"Don't be. Don't be at all. If me moving out on my own brings out the worst in my brother, then this is the way it is, and we each have to take responsibility for that," she noted. "However, we can't blame you because you're supposedly the only harbinger of change."

"Well, it'd be nice if I'm not blamed for it," she agreed, "but I'm not sure your brother is capable of seeing clarity on this issue."

"No, I'm not sure he is either," Giada noted sadly. "But I do thank you for calling and talking to me. At least you are listening to me. He definitely isn't, coming up with every explanation but the real one. I don't know that he'll ever understand, but, hey, maybe one day my brother will come to his senses."

"And what do I do?" Margaret asked, with such sadness in her tone.

"What do you want to do?" Giada asked, hoping that Margaret wouldn't give up on her brother. "He's a good man. He's just …" She frowned and added, "You know what? I think it's just a case of he's feeling the weight of being the eldest and the only male and feeling like he's responsible for keeping us together. But he's not willing to see that his actions are pushing us apart."

"Sounds like a guy, doesn't it?" Margaret teased.

There was just enough laughter in her voice to make Giada feel better. "Well, I wouldn't want to say that outright to my brother," Giada muttered, "but sometimes it does make me wonder."

"Of course it does," Margaret stated, "and I'm happy to stand by whatever it is that you want to do."

"Thank you. I've decided I'll move into an apartment here at work. They have a place available for me to live here, and that's huge."

"Wow, do they?" Margaret sounded delighted at the offer, but Giada wondered if it was because she'd get the house to herself.

"Yes," Giada replied. "Hathaway House has residences here for the staff, and I've been offered one, so it seemed like an opportune time to accept."

"Absolutely," she said.

"And I'll enjoy it here, with free room and board, no commute," she explained, now with laughter in her voice. "It would be the first time I don't have the heavy hand of my brother overseeing what I do."

"Ouch," Margaret replied. "That's one of the things that I do worry about because he becomes too autocratic, and I won't be able to handle it."

"Yep, I hear you, and I'm sorry that that has become a concern, but obviously it's understandable. You should talk to him about that, about your need to have your own business too." Giada added quietly, "I am at work, so I do need to go though."

"Sorry," she said immediately. "I'll talk to you later." And, with that, Margaret hung up.

Giada sat here for a long moment, worried that her brother would lose the few people who were really important to him—all because of his stubbornness. And yet Giada couldn't do a whole lot about it. If he chose to order Giada and Margaret about, and he pushed away both of the women in his life, what was Giada supposed to do? She couldn't change him. That was up to Francis. And if he didn't learn with Giada and tried that with Margaret? Either he wanted to be bossy or he wanted to share his life with Margaret. He had to choose.

Shaking her head, Giada tried to refocus on work and then realized it was a lost cause. He was her brother, and he loved her—in his own way—but, at the same time, he was frustratingly sexist, like old-world patriarchy.

PERCY HAD BEEN more than happy to see her and to hear that everything was going okay. As much as she hadn't really explained how tough things were, he still got the impression that they weren't great, and that was too bad. Sometimes … sometimes you try to keep things under wraps, and it just doesn't work. And yet Percy was very happy for her sake that she was still sticking by her decision, despite all this antagonism from her sexist brother.

A lot of good should come out of this move for her. When he finally did see her, it was two days later. And that surprised him. But he was trying to be patient and to give her time. Not that she needed time or had asked for time. More like he needed to grant her this transition time because he didn't want to get too impatient with her. But, when he finally did see her, she didn't look so great. She walked into the kitchen, grabbed a coffee without saying anything to anybody, and disappeared.

Almost immediately Percy noted several people exchange worried glances. And he realized that things were not going the way Giada had hoped. He didn't know what to do about it, and finally, during one of the next sessions with Shane, Percy asked him, "Do you have any suggestions about what to do?"

"We're all talking about her," he admitted quietly. "We're not sure just how bad things are. She has a home here if she wants, and she seems to want it. Also she has friends here, but we really don't want to step in if she doesn't want us to."

"I get that," Percy noted. "I really do. It just, you know, it sucks."

"It does. And that's the part about being a good friend. Do you wait until you're asked to help or do you step in when you finally see there's a problem? You may recognize it. But she's not there yet."

"And I don't want to step in too early *or* too late," he stated bluntly. "She's a good person, and whatever that jerk brother of hers is doing to her, she doesn't deserve it."

"And who are you? Defender of the innocent and the weak?" Shane sported a big grin.

"Absolutely. I took an oath to my country. Only because of an accident was I sidelined in the first place," he noted quietly. "But to see anybody hurt another person, like she's obviously hurting, is unacceptable."

"That's true," Shane agreed, "but you also have to realize that her pain could very well be because she's leaving him too. Don't forget. She's looked after him for a very long time. So there's an emotional trauma as well. We don't know that the brother is doing anything outside of making her life miserable."

Percy snapped at that. "And *that* shouldn't even be allowed."

"No, maybe not, but they do have to work out some things themselves," Shane suggested, with a word of warning. "And you need to understand that stress will not be your friend. And, if you can't discern how to separate yourself from that kind of stress," Shane pointed out, "we'll have issues too."

"Why?" Percy asked.

"Because you're not progressing this week. And I'm afraid it's because you're spending way-too-much time worrying about her."

Percy frowned at Shane. "It's not wrong to worry about a friend, especially if you're afraid that they're in serious trouble."

"Absolutely," he agreed. "And believe me. We're all keeping an eye on her. But you also have to look after yourself."

Percy didn't like hearing that, but Shane wouldn't listen to any kind of argument.

"No," Shane snapped. "Stop. This isn't just about her. This is also about you. It's also about why you're here. It's also about you making the most of being here. And I get that you're worried. I really do. But, at the same time, we have to ensure that your focus is on you, above all else. And believe me. We have separated various people because it wasn't working out in the best interests of the patient, so that's … if I see that this is not something that you can control," Shane explained, "we will separate you."

Percy started at Shane in horror. "Seriously?"

Shane was adamant. "It's for *your* greater good. You got a bed here, a place here. Now earn it. So keep focused, and, if we need your help with Giada, we'll ask, or if you feel like something is seriously wrong with Giada, we'll listen. But other than that, work." And he forced Percy back to doing more reps.

By the time today's rehab workout was over, Percy was partially pissed, and, at the same time, oddly enough, he admired the fact that Shane had tackled Percy's focus problem head-on.

Percy groaned as he settled on his bed. "You really got yourself in a pickle now." Because, of course, he cared about Giada, and he didn't want to see her hurt. He sent her a text. **Thinking of you.**

She sent back a quick response. **Ditto. I'll be okay.**

And he left it at that.

When he did finally see her, it was several days later. And she didn't look to be too upset. He called her over. She smiled and joined him, giving him a quick hug. "Are you all right?" he asked.

Immediately her smile brightened, and she nodded. "Apparently lots of people are worried about me," she quipped lightly.

"Have you moved here yet?"

"Not quite there yet," she noted. "There's more to my stuff than I expected."

"Do you have to do it all now?"

"No," she admitted quietly, "but I would like to."

He could only be happy with that. "Have lunch with me today?" he asked impulsively.

She looked at him, obviously pleased. "I'd like that."

He smiled. "So would I. It seems like so long since we spent any time together." But then that made him sound like a schoolboy who couldn't handle a separation, and that's the last thing he wanted because that would just bring up, part and parcel, the reminder of her brother.

"Well, that's not what I intended to do," she stated. "Life's just throwing me some curves."

"I think life does that on purpose," he replied, with a deliberate, lighthearted attitude. "Just to see if we can handle it."

"Most of the time I'd have said we could," she murmured. "And then, every once in a while, there's a situation where you get thrown for a loop."

"As long as you realize that the loops come and the loops go," he noted, "and not everything in life is quite so black-and-white."

She looked at him, smiled. "I needed that. Thank you. Hopefully I'll move in within a few days."

"You said that over a week ago."

"I know," she admitted. "But it's important to me that I clear out all this stuff that my parents had saved and say goodbye to the whole family-unit problem at the same time," she explained, "so it's a little bit tough."

"I think people are just worried your brother'll be difficult."

"And so am I," she agreed. "Those are all valid concerns. His fiancée's involved now too." She shrugged. "But what am I supposed to do? He is who he is, and, if he's not prepared to understand and to make some allowances for his own issues and for mine and even Margaret's, then we all have some problems."

"Of course you've got problems," he said, with a smile, "but, in a family, they're supposed to be ones who you can talk about this stuff with as adults and work it out somehow."

"And I hope so," she stated. "I really do." And then she turned and waved. "I'll see you at noon."

With that, he had to be satisfied.

Chapter 12

G IADA CAME HOME that night to find her brother sitting in the living room, waiting for her. With her heart in her throat, she sat down on the couch. "Hey, how you doing?"

"I talked to Margaret today," he said, his voice dark.

"Good." Giada's phone buzzed at that point. She looked down to see a text from Margaret, saying she was on her way. "Was it a good conversation?"

"No," he replied, "it wasn't."

"Ah, well, I'm sorry. I hope there's nothing serious wrong between the two of you."

"Of course not," he snapped. "It would take a lot more than this to rock that boat."

She wasn't sure what *this* was but didn't like his inference that anything to do with him was solid and good, but anything to do with Giada or Margaret was not. "So what's the problem?" she asked, refusing to be intimidated.

"I don't want you to leave," he stated.

"That's too bad because I'm leaving. It's my decision, after all." Matter of fact, she had most of her things packed up, ready to go. She had taken in quite a few loads already. But hadn't made the final move.

"I don't think it's right. I don't think Papa would agree."

"I don't think Papa would have any say in the matter,"

she argued, "and I know Mama would agree." It was hard to refute that. But, of course, he would try.

"But Papa's rule was law."

"Papa's rule *was* law," she repeated. "And that was a long time ago. Papa is not here, and his law is no longer." She added, "I get that you're trying to reenact that whole old-school family dynamic, but it won't work. Not with me. Not with Margaret either, so keep that in mind. I'm leaving. You're getting married. You're getting to start a whole new life, and I want to start my new life."

He looked at her in surprise.

She nodded. "Did you think I just wanted to sit here and look after you for the rest of my life? Did you think it was my *duty*? No wonder you don't appreciate all I've done for you over the years. You think like some employer, not like my brother. And did you think I haven't had other opportunities to meet people and to go places?" she asked, looking at him and shaking her head. "Did you really think nobody was interested in me? Or could be interested in me?"

He frowned, opened his mouth, then closed it.

"My God," she said, "if you have been thinking that way the whole time, you're barking up the wrong tree."

"Then why haven't you started your *new life* before now?"

"Because, like you, it was comfortable here," she admitted quietly. "Like you, it was family. It was just the two of us, and it was what we knew for many years, and it was good," she noted, "but it's not good anymore, and it's not what we have anymore because you have Margaret now."

"So it is about Margaret."

"No, of course it's not about Margaret," she said, raising both hands. "I love her. She's beautiful, and she's good for you. But she also deserves the respect of being able to have her own house without a carry-on person, particularly when the third wheel doesn't want to stay here. You can't keep me here as a prisoner, even though I'm sure in your mind you've probably contemplated the idea because that's definitely something Papa would do. Do you think it's great that he tried to stop Mama from working, that when she wanted to take classes that he wouldn't let her?"

"Well of course, she didn't need to."

"It had nothing to do with *need*," Giada explained quietly. "Mama *wanted* to. She wanted to learn more about the world. She wanted to take geography classes. What was wrong with that?" she asked him.

He frowned. "Nothing," he replied cautiously.

"Exactly. Nothing. It was all about control. It was all about Papa keeping Mama under his thumb, that he didn't want her to get any broader in education and move away from him in any way," she stated. "How was that good? How was that a life for her? She let him do it because she loved him, and she knew how much it tormented him to think that she would do anything that would lead to her leaving him."

"Of course she wouldn't have left him," he said in disgust. "Why would you even bring that up?"

"Because it's what Papa was afraid of," she murmured. "And, for that reason alone, you need to understand that I don't want to stay here anymore. I'm happy that you've found somebody else, and I'm happy that I get to step away and have a life for myself now."

"Did you really just stay for me?"

"Partly, yes," she admitted. "I stayed for you because of you, for you, and for myself. Because like I said, it was easy.

But I want something more," she stated. "I want my own marriage. I want my own family, and, yes, there is potential for that out there for me," she snapped, "no matter how ugly you may think I am."

"It's got nothing to do with ugliness, and you know it," he replied, "but it'll be hard to find anybody who's good enough."

"Well, *you* don't get to make that choice," she said, with a word of warning. "I know that, in your mind, Papa would accept or reject any choices of mine, but that time has come and gone, and it won't come back again. I love you dearly, bro, but you won't make those decisions for me."

He frowned again.

She added, "And, if you're honest, you don't want the weight of that on you. You don't want to be responsible, should things go wrong." He opened his mouth, and she shook her head. "Nope, we're not doing this. Now I am still going through the stuff in my room and what Mama and Papa stored away in the spare bedroom, but I should be done in another day or two. I'd like to leave on good terms. But, regardless of the terms," she declared, "I *am* leaving."

"Do you already have somebody?" he asked abruptly.

Immediately her mind went to Percy. "I really like somebody, yes," she replied. "Is it good enough to sustain through the years? I don't know," she admitted, "but I hope so. Will I let you meet him? Eventually but not for a while."

"Did you meet him at that place?" he asked, his voice hard.

"Watch what you say," she ordered, standing now. "Because *that place* is not only where I work but it's where the people I care about live and work too. Most of the patients had military careers and are good and honorable and brave people."

"Military," he said, with disgust.

She warned him again. "Remember. Don't go there. Just because Papa was against it doesn't mean you have to be."

"You've changed," he noted abruptly.

"No, I haven't actually, but I am coming out of my skin," she explained, "and that's a good thing. Because I spent way too much time not listening to all the things that I wanted to do with my life, but now I am. And I will make these changes."

"And I won't stop you," he replied, growling. "But I'd feel better if I knew where you were going and that you would be okay."

"I've got an apartment at my work," she replied. "It's always been available to me, but I just never really had a reason or the inclination to live there too, but now I do."

"Because of him?"

"No, not because of him," she noted quietly, "because of me. Because you're getting married. And I want Margaret to be happy. And she won't be happy if she steps into a family full of strife, where I'm being forced to stay because *you* think I don't have any other options," she repeated. "I'm looking forward to this. This is a good thing. For you and for me." He wanted to argue, but there wasn't a whole lot he could say. She shook her head. "Now I'll go upstairs and keep working and then I'll start dinner."

"I'm going out for dinner," he stated, "with Margaret."

"Good. Enjoy."

And, with that, Giada dashed up the stairs, quite over-joyed that she wouldn't even be cooking dinner tonight. Pretty quickly she would be eating at Hathaway's kitchen for a while. She didn't know how long that would work out, but it was hard to imagine any better place to go to while she adapted to the new status quo in her life. This really was a good thing. And she was so excited about her future. Now all she had to do was make sure that everybody at the job understood that it was okay because apparently, when something happened to one of them, everybody got involved.

"Almost like it's family all over again," she murmured. Really who could argue with that? Because they were good people. She already knew that, and she was blessed to have them care. And, with that, she started the last bout of packing. She was really looking forward to spending time at the center in the evenings. And she thought, with joy, at the pool. Life couldn't get much better than that.

TWO DAYS LATER Percy sat outside, beside the pool, after a particularly hard session with Shane, when he saw her driving around one of the apartment areas and pulling up to the side. He watched in surprise and joy, as she started to unpack the last of the stuff that she had. She saw him, waved, and yelled out, "I'll be over in a minute."

He smiled and waited. When she came to join him, she had on a bathing suit. He laughed. "I didn't even think of that," he admitted, "but I guess you get the benefits of living here too, don't you?"

"Believe me. I checked on that first," she said in a teasing voice. "It shouldn't be just you who gets to have the pool." She laughed at her own joke.

He nodded. "Be my guest. I've just come out here too."

"Are you done for the day?" she asked.

"I am. At least for now." And she took off her cover-up, and he was treated to the sight of her fit and beautiful body, right before she dove into the water, completely casual and unconcerned.

When she came up on the other side, she looked at him and asked, "Why didn't I do this a long time ago?"

He burst out laughing. "That'll be a question you ask yourself a lot in the coming weeks," he suggested. "Because really, there was no need to *not* move here."

"Maybe, but sometimes I think things have to happen the way they're meant to," she murmured. "And so maybe my timing on this is all good." She hopped out and sat down beside him. "You going to stay out here or are you coming in the pool?"

"I'll rest right now," he replied. Immediately she frowned. He shook his head. "I'm fine, but I've already done quite a few laps, and I have to preserve my energy."

"Of course you do," she agreed. "Whereas I have more than enough to get rid of, so I'll see you in a few minutes."

And she dove back under and started doing laps. He watched with joy, realizing just how much having her around would be to his benefit too. Not only would it keep Shane off his back, but it would give Percy something to look forward to at the end of every day.

Life had never looked better.

Chapter 13

H ER CAR LOADED with the last of her things, Giada turned back to her brother, who stood in the open front doorway, his arms over his chest.

"This is a good thing," she repeated gently. He frowned and looked away. "That's fine. You don't have to accept it. But it *is* a good thing." She looked at Margaret at her brother's side and smiled. "Be happy for me," she said to them both.

Margaret immediately nodded. "I am," she replied. "You're right. It is a good thing."

Her brother glanced at his fiancée sharply.

Margaret turned and looked at him, her hands on her hips. "It *is* a good thing. And it's not right for you to fight her on this," she said pointedly. And, with that, she walked over and gave Giada a big hug. "Enjoy and make sure you come back often."

"Will do." And, with a smile and a wave, Giada got in her vehicle and headed to work. It was a Saturday, but she'd been bringing multiple loads consistently for a couple days now. She didn't realize how much she had that she needed to bring with her, hadn't even thought that she would have so much stuff to move. But then, she'd apparently been fooling herself the whole time. With each box she had filled, it amazed her because she'd sorted and tossed, sorted and tossed, and yet still had so much left to go through. It took her way longer than she had expected, but she was done now.

It had been an emotional journey in many ways, and that had been hard, sorting through a lot of her parents' belongings and keepsakes, a lot of her grandparents' things even. They were obviously a family of collectors. The good thing was, she'd had had copies of various photos made for herself and had left those originals behind for her brother to deal with, along with the memories of his childhood and teen years, and she'd only had to deal with her own memorabilia. And that had been plenty. Matter of fact, it had been too much. It had been an emotional tossing and turning. And she realized just how belated her moving out actually was.

She'd held back her own growth, and she wasn't happy about that, sighing out loud. It was kind of sad really. She shook off that thought as she parked outside of her new home. She pulled herself up out of the car, already tired from previous trips today. Or maybe she had new fears about putting herself *here* because not only was this her workplace but now her home. If she lost one, she lost both. And that would be rough too.

Nothing that she had really thought about ahead of time, but she shrugged. It was time to grow up, time to move out, time to move on. She would deal with her problems as they showed up. Yes, she could plan for eventualities, but she would not worry needlessly. Most of her worries never led anywhere. She had to remember that. *Remember. Don't worry.*

"Do you always talk to yourself?" came a teasing voice. She turned to see Percy in his wheelchair, sitting right here, almost waiting for her. It was perfect. She walked over, bent down, and gave him a gentle hug. "I know you didn't need that," she noted, "but I did."

Immediately his arms went around her and gripped her firmly, hugging her back. "Anytime you need a hug," he said, "I'm here."

She smiled, stepped back, and asked, "And how are you? I haven't had time to even visit lately. That pool visit was two nights ago, then I had more packing to do."

"But you're here now," he noted, with a motion of his hand. "Or are you?" His gaze was intense, as he studied her.

She nodded. "Absolutely. I'm here now. My brother is still adapting. His fiancée is thrilled for me, happy for herself, a little worried maybe for herself," she said, laughing. "Because my brother isn't all that easy a person to get along with, and I think this has shown her a few issues that should be dealt with before she moves in. I think it's a good thing for them to sort it out now, before the wedding." She sighed. "For me? Well, I'll be a little emotional for a bit, but I'll be fine."

He gave her the gentlest of smiles. "You want a hand unloading?" She looked at him, looked at her stuff, and realized that all the doors were wheelchair accessible. "Sure," she said. "Why not?"

And she quickly filled his lap with stuff, even hooking some bags on the back of his wheelchair. When he finally laughingly told her to stop, that he couldn't move when so weighted down, she grinned and watched as he carefully maneuvered his way inside. By the time she had another load in her arms and brought it behind him, she was there to help him unload and then went back outside again. "That wheelchair is pretty handy," she noted admiringly.

"Oh, I don't think they thought it should be used for this purpose right off the bat," he teased. "But honestly it's nice to do something."

She stopped, looked at him, and then nodded quietly. "Again it's finding that sweet spot, isn't it? Finding the point where you can be a help and not feel like a burden. *Huh.*" She nodded. "I feel like I'm doing that myself right now."

"You are," he agreed. "I don't think you were ever a burden in your mind and probably not in your brother's mind either."

"But the fact of the matter is, I was," she noted quietly. "Even though neither of us was thinking that way, the truth of the matter was, he was concerned about my future, wondering how to make me stay in the house, look after him, cook and clean for him, so not to change things that he was comfortable with. Yet, at the same time, also knowing that he wanted me to have a secure future."

Percy nodded in understanding.

"You know what? Conflicting emotions were all over the place," she stated, with a smile. "Still are. And it's good. It's all good because we're growing and working our way through this," she admitted cheerfully.

And she knew he heard the tears in the back of her throat, but he was polite enough not to say anything, and she appreciated it. When they were finally done, he looked at her and asked, "You know it's dinnertime, right?"

"Good thing," she said, straightening up slowly and stretching. "I'm starved. It'll be nice to have my own kitchen as well, so that I can cook on my own sometime too."

"And I think you can also ask for meals in advance," he noted. When she looked at him, puzzled, he shrugged. "I saw Stan walk out with what looked like leftovers packaged up in containers."

"Oh, interesting," she said, looking toward the main building. "I'll have to check that out a little bit more. Because you know …" And then she laughed. "I have heard Dennis packs a wonderful picnic too, made to be enjoyed outside around this place."

Percy nodded, considering that. "Wow, you know that would be …" He looked at the land surrounding them. "That would be awesome."

"Right? A little privacy, a chance to get out in Mother Nature, enjoy all the animals and the gloriousness that's here." She beamed. "I can see that being a future goal."

"Count me in," he said, with feeling.

She laughed. "Of course. We'll have to talk to Dennis and see what we can work out."

"I think Dennis is a bit of a matchmaker," Percy noted, with a gentle charm.

"I think they all are here," she added, with a sly look, "in case you haven't noticed that yet."

"I have heard mention of it. Aaron's coming back next week too," he stated abruptly.

She looked at him in surprise. "Awesome." Then she stopped and nodded. "I forgot that he was a good friend of yours."

"We served together," he stated. "He's the one who convinced me to come here."

"And I'm glad he did. I wouldn't have met you otherwise."

He stopped, gave a gentle sigh, and said, "You're really good at that."

She looked at him and laughed. "I'm really good at what?"

"At saying things that don't have to be prompted but come from heart," he explained. "Nice things. I'm not sure of the last time anybody said anything really nice to me," he murmured. "You spend so much time in rehab, where you know that people are being paid to shuffle you from one medical personnel to another, but sometimes it doesn't really come from the heart. It doesn't really come from genuine niceness," he noted. "It's more like just a job."

"Well, I'm never just about the job, even when at work," she declared. "I'm thinking how I can make it better for the staff and the patients too. Not that the others aren't doing that as well, but just … I guess my position makes that easier though. My job's not like what the medical staff deals with, having their doctor-patient priorities. I'm just the one who buys the toilet paper."

He burst out laughing at that. "You have no idea how important that job of yours is then," he replied cheekily.

She grinned. "It's become a bit of a running joke around the place, I think," she admitted.

"Yeah, *running* all at the wrong times too, I'm sure," he teased, cracking up with laughter.

She smiled. "And I can see you'll perpetuate that same issue, won't you?"

"You know something? I just might." Laughing, he asked, "You ready to go get food?"

"Absolutely. Yet it feels kind of weird," she added, as they walked over to the main building.

"Weird how?" he murmured, looking at it her.

"It's the first time that I'm having a meal, where I'm allowed to be here."

"Were you not allowed to eat here before?"

"You know what? That's part of the mind-set that I was

trying to adjust to because, of course, I *was* allowed. Dani kept telling me that," she explained. "I just didn't feel like I had the right."

"Ah," he said, "and that's a very different thing."

"I know," she admitted, "and it's such a weird feeling to really *know* that this is where I belong now. This is where I get my meals. I mean, after years and years of just cooking every meal for my brother," she said, "it almost feels like a release from a life sentence."

At that, he burst out laughing again.

She grinned. "See? And I don't have to worry about you taking that the wrong way."

"Nope, not at all," he agreed, "because anybody who has to cook a meal every day regardless would seem like a life sentence to them. There is such a thing as restaurants and picnics for a reason."

"And yet none of that was of any interest to my brother," she noted, "and, of course, I was still doing it because I promised my mother I would." She raised both hands, shaking her head. "That's the problem when your mother is sick and when she's worried about her little boy. You would promise anything to make her feel better, but then you're obligated because of that promise. And that's where I got stuck."

"And now you're unstuck," he reminded her gently.

"Yes. I don't even know what to do with myself now," she said. "It just feels like so much has opened up."

"It has," he agreed, "but there are also challenges to being here full-time."

She stopped, looked at him, and asked, "Like what?"

"Well, you have to realize Hathaway House is a self-contained world unto itself, and you'll need to physically make some changes in order to ensure that you don't become housebound. Yet you also need boundaries, so that your work life doesn't take over your personal life."

She nodded. "You know what? Those are two really good points. I hadn't considered that."

He smiled. "Stick with me, baby, and we'll go far."

Laughing, the two of them walked and wheeled into the dining room to see a line just starting to form. He raced forward, took a spot in line. She caught up with him and said, "You're moving pretty fast in that thing."

"I'm doing better," he agreed. "I've got a long way to go, but, as of today, things feel mighty good."

MATTER OF FACT, Giada and Percy were starting to feel better than *mighty good*. And that same sense of euphoria lasted well through the next week and the week after that. They didn't have every meal together, but, when they could, they managed to sit down together. And slowly the circle of people around them widened, as they were welcomed into other groups. About a week later, she sat outside on the deck, hidden ever-so-slightly out of the way from the sun, when she heard Shane call to her.

"How are you doing these days?" he asked her. "Fully adapted to being here?"

She smiled and then laughed. "Absolutely. I should have done it a lot earlier," she murmured. "It's been great."

"Good," he said. "And I see that you and Percy are spending a lot of time together."

At first she continued to smile, but then she frowned. "And hopefully there's nothing against that."

"No, not at all," he replied. "Just like everything, keep it in check, and move slowly."

"Right. I remember that. Nothing's allowed to impact the healing of the people here."

"Absolutely," he agreed. "But when we see people who are super happy together, it really does help the healing here, both physically and emotionally. And not just for you and Percy, but for the others who witness it as well. Each miracle leading to more miracles."

"And that's all good news," she stated, "because I'm really enjoying spending time with Percy. He's a nice man."

Shane heard the smile in her voice when she had said that. "I just wanted to …" And then he hesitated.

"Just wanted to what? You mean, what are my intentions?" she asked on a teasing note.

He burst out laughing. "No, not at all. I'm not worried about that." Then he stopped and asked, "Your brother was a project, right?"

"Well, that's one way to look at it," she agreed, "but not a terribly nice way to look at it—or at least he wouldn't appreciate me calling him a project. But you know what? It was a responsibility that I took on, yes."

"Okay," Shane said, "so don't take this the wrong way, but I should remind you that Percy's not a project for you to take on either. Okay?"

A shocked gasp escaped before she could stop it. "Is that what it looks like?" she asked in a hushed whisper.

"I don't know that it is or isn't," he stated. "It occurred to me, as things were moving quickly with you two, and I know that you just relinquished your responsibility for your brother. I don't want you to …" He winced. "I am literally checking in with you to ensure that this is something you keep an eye on. I don't want you to think that because Percy needs help right now that your relationship is based on that current need. He will heal and get better and better. He won't need the services of Hathaway House for long."

PERCY OVERHEAD THEIR discussion as he headed their way. Shane had said something else, but he'd lowered his voice, and Percy couldn't hear that last part. He frowned at Shane's earlier words. That *project* scenario had never occurred to him, but it should have. Matter of fact, it pissed off Percy to even consider such a thing, but now it had to be considered.

It's not that Percy wasn't worthy of a relationship. He looked down at the wheelchair and winced. Generally his self-confidence was enough to buffet that kind of negative thinking. Sure, he'd been there with the doubts and had gotten quite distraught over a ton of upset in his life, but he didn't think he was quite there right now anymore.

Yet to think, to consider that she might think of him as a project or as needing her and, therefore, Percy could be considered just a replacement for her brother was not something Percy wanted to even think about.

Only now that the words had been spoken, even though he wasn't intended to hear them, Percy couldn't put them back in the box. Slowly, instead of meeting up with her, he slunk out of the dining room and back to his room. He needed time to think. He sent her a quick text. **Going to spend time in my room tonight. Not feeling so great.**

And he hoped that she'd leave it at that. When she sent him a sad face and then a heart, he realized just how involved the two of them were. And was it a good involvement, or was it a not-so-good involvement?

Were they together for the right reasons?

He desperately wanted it to be a good and healthy relationship. He desperately wanted it to be real. But just as he couldn't afford to make that kind of mistake, neither could she, not a second time. She'd spent a lot of time at her brother's side for her brother's sake. But it was time for her to do what she needed to do for herself. And the same went for Percy.

That was something he would now have to sit and think about, even though it was the last thing that he even wanted to contemplate. Sad, uneasy, he brought out his laptop and typed out the crazy thoughts that churned through his mind. He didn't know what to think anymore. Didn't know how to even react. It's like something in his world had just ... shattered. It wasn't her fault. It wasn't his fault.

It was a valid point, and he appreciated the fact that it had been brought up, but, at the same time, he wished to God it had never been brought up. Because who needed that complication, that added stress? There had to be something better in life, at least he could hope so.

And yet, right now, he just wasn't sure where he stood at all.

Chapter 14

I T TOOK GIADA a few days before it finally hit her. It seemed like, for whatever reason, Percy was avoiding her. She thought on it for another day and felt the hurt deep and hot, and then started to get mad. She didn't know what was wrong, but the least he could do was tell her. At the end of her workday, she walked down to his room and knocked. When he didn't answer, she knocked again. She wasn't sure if he was in there or if he assumed it was her and was avoiding her.

She pulled out her phone, texted him. **You're avoiding me. Why?**

She'd always been blunt, had always been somebody who would rather get to the bottom of an issue than have it build. When he didn't respond, she didn't know what to do. Fuming, she turned away again. She sent him another one the next day. **I won't go away. The least you can do is give me an explanation.**

And then it hit her that maybe he was struggling to deal with his own issues. She immediately texted him again. **And I'm so sorry if I find out that there's something seriously wrong. Reach out**, she urged. **I'm here for you.**

Finally he responded. **But the question is, why are you here?**

She stared down at that in confusion. At the same time

Shane popped his head in and looked at her face and laughed. "Well, I don't know what's going on with you," he said, "but that facial expression is worth one thousand words."

"I don't know what either," she noted quietly. "Something weird is going on with Percy this last week," she stated. "He's stopped talking to me and won't tell me what's upsetting him." She looked up at Shane, knowing that her face revealed her fears. "Did he get a diagnosis or something that's really ugly? I know you can't share medical details, but can you tell me in general terms?"

He looked at her in surprise, shook his head. "Not that I know of," he replied cautiously. "It's certainly not what I would have jumped to for a reason either," he noted, looking at her in surprise.

"I know. I know. I'm just …" She threw up her hands. "I'm at a loss. I don't know what I did to upset him, and I don't know why he would be avoiding me right now."

"Maybe give him time?" Shane asked quietly.

"I was doing that," she said. "But now the time has gone on long enough that, well, it's hard to give him any more time, or we may never get past this."

"He has been a little off this last week," Shane agreed, with a nod. "I'm not sure what that's all about. Maybe I'll talk to him tomorrow."

"Could you?" she asked eagerly. "I'm really worried about him."

"You care, don't you?"

"He's the first person I've met in a very long time that makes me feel …" She paused. "I don't even know how to say it—but maybe like *me* again."

"Are you sure it's not because you've just left your

brother and you're into a whole new world?" His question was delivered with a gentle smile.

"Heaven's no." She smiled. "I admit to everything being different now that I'm out of there. I'm really enjoying my newfound freedom. Yet this silence from Percy has kind of kiboshed that whole sense of pursuing my own life on my terms because, well, … I was enjoying spending time with him."

"You didn't move here because of him, right?"

She looked at him in surprise and shook her head. "No. But I would be lying if I said that I *wasn't* looking forward to spending time with him here. Is that wrong?" She looked at Shane, worried. "I don't want him to feel like I'm stalking him or something. But I just really like … *like* him and love spending time with him."

"It's not wrong at all," Shane replied quietly. "Let me see what's up with him tomorrow."

"Good enough." And then she frowned. "And is that even the right thing to do? To let you deal with it? Does that kind of feel like I'm passing the buck to somebody else?"

He laughed. "Sometimes you're overthinking things too."

"Maybe," she said, with relief. "I just want to get to the problem, so we can solve it and can get on with whatever we have going on."

"And maybe he's rethinking?"

She winced. "You know what? Maybe he is, and that would be very hard to take, but I would still rather know."

"Good enough," Shane said. "Doesn't mean he'll talk to me either, but I'll see."

"Good." She left it at that.

WHEN SHANE SHOWED up two days later, he looked at Giada and said, "You really need to talk to him."

"I've been trying to. So what did he say?'

"He wouldn't get into the specifics. But he told me just enough that it made me worry that maybe he overheard something."

She frowned. "What are you talking about?"

"Remember our conversation, where I wanted to make sure that you weren't looking at him as a project?"

She stared at him, her eyes going wide. "Oh my. Seriously?"

"He may have overheard us. Now I don't know for sure. I don't know that that is the problem, but …"

"I have to see him to clear this up with him," she muttered, now standing. "And he'll just make me mad if that is the problem."

"Don't get mad at him," Shane stated. "Remember? All of this is a learning process for him too. He came here with a lot of injuries and is in the middle of a life change. So he'll be feeling more than insecure. Even more than you are."

She looked at him and sank back into her chair. "And that's part of it, isn't it?" she asked. "He's uncertain of me. I'm uncertain of him, and this is where we sit." Moodily, she stared around at her office. "I wonder if I made a mistake moving here. It would be hard to keep seeing him all the time but yet knowing he doesn't care."

"And how would it be to see him all the time and to know that he does care?"

Her face lit up. "That would be fantastic."

"You already know he cares," Shane stated quietly.

"You're not foolish enough to ignore this or to lie to yourself about that, so why don't you work toward solving whatever this problem is, so that you can take the next step—whatever that is."

"Thank you," she said. "I just have to figure out how to make that conversation happen."

"And to not get angry at him, if you're right. Think of it from his point of view. For all you know, he could be stepping away from the relationship *for your own good.*"

"I'm really tired of this 'for my own good' stuff," she muttered.

He laughed out loud. "We're all guilty of that at times. So again, don't get angry at him—because he is, I hate to say it, but he's a male. He's protective. He would want what's best for you, and he would not in any way want to hold you back."

She groaned. "You know this relationship stuff, whether it's family or not, is tough," she lamented.

"It is, but it's also worth working your way through because this is the group who cares for you. And that makes it all worthwhile."

"Well, it might, if I knew what the end result would be." Her stomach was already locked down in knots, thinking that it would be anything other than what she wanted it. "It'll really break my heart if he doesn't feel about me the same way I feel about him," she whispered.

Shane nodded in a commiserating motion. "I get that," he said softly. "So you're probably better off to find out sooner than later."

"And how does one do that when he won't even talk to me?" she exclaimed, staring at Shane.

Shane shrugged. "You could waylay him, but, if you do

it in an ugly way, he won't like it."

"No. No, he sure won't, and I can't put him on the spot because then he'll take it the wrong way too. Somehow I have to get him to see me and to talk to me," she said quietly. "Let me think on it."

And, with that, Shane disappeared.

Which was a good thing because she wanted to just lay her head down and cry. How had it come to this? What had he heard or come up with in his mind that made this so hard for them to talk about it? Determinedly she went back to work, but she let things noodle around in the back of her brain. There had to be some way to reach him. Some way that he wouldn't take offense.

IT WAS HARD for Percy to get through the next few days. It had been a tough week, but he'd been on a self-righteous kick. *It was good for her, better for him, to be apart right now.* And instead, after talking to Shane and refusing to discuss what was going on, Percy realized that maybe he was being a little foolish. Maybe acting too much like her sexist brother. And what Percy was doing affected other people here—the healing element that was priority number one here—and that was not acceptable.

Shane had warned him that, if there was any kind of disturbance in his own healing, then Shane would have to make changes. And Percy definitely got the impression that that change would likely involve Giada. And that wouldn't be fair. Percy didn't know exactly what Shane's threat would entail, but it was a point in time that Percy didn't even want to get to.

Giada was a special woman, and he really cared for her. Was he being a fool? A lovesick fool? Was he overthinking this? Was he worrying about something that didn't deserve to be worried about? Was it wrong for her to even see him as a project? Maybe she was the kind of person who set things as a goal. Get him walking or get him talking or getting him on a date.

He didn't know.

Because he hadn't given her a change to explain.

It all felt so foolish now that he sat here, a whole different thought forming in his head. Why hadn't he considered this a week ago and just talked to Giada about it, before it got to be such a big deal?

As he sat here, fuming and upset, he looked outside and desperately needed to get out there. He'd even avoided the pool because chances were good that she would be there. What were the chances that she'd been avoiding it too? He would love to meet her again in the pool.

That's where they spent a lot of time together. Both of them were water rats, and, with her thoroughly enjoying the amenities that the job and now the location afforded her, he'd been so happy for her. The same as he'd been happy for himself, when he realized the pool and hot tub were available to him and all the patients. Frustrated and angry, he headed out onto the deck outside the dining room, looking outside. He was still in the wheelchair, had been warned it would be another few weeks before he graduated to crutches.

But he was stronger now. He looked out at the pasture and wondered. Behind him he heard Dennis talking to somebody. Then Dennis called out to Percy. He twisted to watch, as Dennis walked closer. "Hey what?" Percy asked Dennis.

Dennis gave him a knowing look. "Trouble in romance land, huh?"

"Was that what it was?" he asked quietly. "I guess I didn't see that for sure."

"Then your eyes weren't open," Dennis stated bluntly.

He winced. "I guess everybody's talking about it, huh?"

"Nope, not yet, but, if you aren't interested, then you're better off to let her go," Dennis stated. "She deserves somebody who cares about her. And not just somebody who cares *for* her."

At that odd phrasing, Percy looked over at Dennis and frowned.

Dennis nodded. "She's had a few tough years—a lot of tough years actually—but she's a good person, with a good heart."

"I guess I was just afraid that she was only with me as a replacement for her brother."

Dennis looked at him in surprise. "Do you want to explain that?"

"She always looked after her brother, and now, without that responsibility anymore, I felt like she was kind of at loose ends and potentially looking at me as a replacement project."

Dennis stopped, thought about it for a long moment, and shook his head. "It never even occurred to me that somebody would think that," he said, "but the human mind constantly amazes me in how twisted up and convoluted it can make something otherwise so very simple."

"Is it simple?" Percy asked. "I've been bashing myself up for the last few days, thinking I was being an idiot."

"You *are* being an idiot," Dennis agreed instantly.

Percy snorted. "Well, thanks for that," he muttered.

"Hey, stupid is as stupid does, and I've always been one to call a spade a spade. That woman cares. I get that you probably still have some things to work out, things to talk out, and she probably does too," he muttered. "But don't ever mistake real emotion for the fake stuff. She cares. It's up to you and Giada to define how you want that caring to show."

"Sounds simple when you say it that way."

"Heck no, it's not simple," Dennis exclaimed. "None of this dealing with humans is simple, but why should that stop you? Anything worthwhile is worth doing and doing right," he stated. "You care. She cares. I'd like to think the pathway forward for any couple would be simple, but apparently it never is. Look. Why don't I make you a picnic, and you get out there? Spend some time communing with the horses, thinking about life, thinking about what changes you could make, pondering what you want to do."

"A picnic." Percy nodded and smiled. "You know what? We often said that we would have a picnic."

"Well, right now you can do it, alone or with Giada, while you assess where and what you want out of life," he stated. "Go on, get to the elevator, and I'll have something done up for you and will meet you there."

By the time Percy made it in his wheelchair to the elevator, he was surprised to see Dennis standing there. "Now that was fast."

"It is, but, then again, I'm good at what I do," Dennis stated, with a beaming smile. He placed the basket of food in his lap and said, "Now get out there. You should visit the animals more. Another thing you need to switch up and change," he noted. "Stan will probably come out and see you, when you're out with the horses anyway. Good time to chat with him and reconsider the values of life. Nothing like injured animals to help remind you what you can and can't do in your own world." And, with that, Dennis pushed the button for the elevator to bring it to Percy's level and left.

By the time Percy was outside, he saw Stan, leaning over a fence. Percy wheeled over there, caught the guy's eye. Percy looked up and smiled and said, "I'm Percy, in case you forgot. We met earlier."

Stan nodded. "Giada has spoken about you many times."

At that, Percy's face fell.

"Yep, I heard about trouble in paradise," Stan noted, even with a smile. "That's okay. You can commune with the animals. They'll make you feel better about things." He looked at the picnic basket in his lap and pointed. "Perfect. If you're lucky, she might even join you."

"I don't think she wants anything to do with me right now," he replied quietly. "And why would she? I haven't even returned her calls."

"Now we've got hurt feelings involved too," Stan noted, with a sage nod of his head. "But I have faith in humanity. I have faith that you are capable of fixing whatever it is that's gone wrong," he murmured. "That is, if you care to." As he studied Percy's face, he nodded. "Obviously you care." He whistled.

As Percy turned, a huge black Newfoundlander with three legs came to join them.

"Take Helga with you," Stan said. "She needs a walk."

Percy stared at her huge welcoming eyes.

"This girl's got a lot of energy, and I haven't had a chance to take her out. So head on down over in that corner and let her go with you—if you don't mind, that is?" Stan asked, raising an eyebrow.

"I'd be honored," Percy said, with a smile.

"Good answer," he murmured.

Moving slowly and wheeling himself at a pace that Percy could handle, Helga walking beside him, the two of them working their way down the path to a spot that looked quite appealing. He reached a flat area that looked out at the horses and said, "Well, Helga, what do you think?"

Helga woofed once and walked toward the horses; a big midnight-black one walked up, and the two sniffed each other, as if they were longtime friends.

As Percy sat here, he felt some of the loneliness creeping in on him. It wasn't supposed to be like this; it was supposed to be not just him. She was supposed to be sharing this picnic with him. How had it gotten to this point?

He shook his head, feeling the pain of his fears creeping in on him. He'd been an idiot. The least he could have done was spoken to her about his concerns, but he hadn't. He'd gotten upset and angry, had shut down, and that was as far as he got.

"Stupid," he muttered out loud.

A gentle voice beside him asked, "Stupid, why?"

Percy looked up to see Giada walking toward him. She carried two cups of coffee. He looked at her hands and said, "I don't know why you would be bringing me one of those. I don't deserve it for not speaking to you."

She stopped in surprise and then continued to walk ever-so-quietly. "I don't know about *deserve*," she said. "That word is not one I tend to use very much."

"Maybe not, but I think it probably should be used for me."

"*Ah*. I'm not really into hating. I'm not really into arguing, and I'm sure as heck not into blaming," she stated. "But may I sit?"

"Sure," he said. "I don't know what's in this picnic basket that Dennis sent with me, but you're welcome to share it with me."

"I don't need anything," she replied, with a wave of her hand. "I can always get something later."

"And that's the trouble," he noted. "You're almost too selfless."

"Can somebody be *too* selfless?"

"I don't know. I guess. Maybe. I don't know anymore," he said, frowning. "You've got me all twisted up, inside out, and backward."

"And that was never my intention," she replied, her voice sad.

He looked over at her, hating to see a glistening tear in her eye. "Don't cry. Oh, please, don't cry."

She brushed her eyes. "It's not tears. Something's in my eye."

But he didn't believe her. Still, he looked at her and realized that, of the two of them, he was the one who needed to start. "I'm sorry."

Startled, she looked up. "Okay. Maybe you could explain why?" she asked hopefully. "It would be a lot easier to understand the sudden silence if I had any inkling as to what brought it on."

"You didn't do anything," he replied. "It's me."

She winced at that. "You know what? I've had a few relationships in life, and too often I've heard that same phrasing. *It's not you. It's me.* Which really means, it *is* me, and you don't want to tell me."

At that, he looked at her in surprise. "That's not what I

meant, and I'm not like your old boyfriends," he stated, "but I'm just the biggest fool because anybody who let you go was an idiot."

She stared at him in complete astonishment, and he watched as the tears collected in her eyes again.

"And I mean it from the bottom of my heart when I say, *I'm sorry*. I heard something. It upset me. I got up on my high horse. I figured that you would be better off without me, or I'd be better off without you. By this point in time I really don't know which way I was twisting it around to … justify it somehow. Then it became really hard to cross the divide again."

"You really mean to apologize?"

"I really am sorry."

"Again that's not an explanation, but I do … I would like more," she corrected herself.

"I overheard you and Shane," he stated, "something about me being a project. I couldn't hear all of it, and I'm afraid I just heard enough of it to get myself into deep trouble."

She stared at him, and her shoulders sagged. "Shane mentioned something just the other day that he was afraid you had heard part of that conversation. And I have to admit, it never occurred to me that, if you had heard it, that it would have upset you because why?" she asked. "There was no need for worry or anger. But I do understand that, if you only heard some of it, then maybe it would upset you. First off, let's clear the air. I don't see you as a project. I don't need a project. I don't want a project. I feel like I've had lots of my time spent looking after others or being in service to others. It *is* a part of my innate nature. I don't see that as a wrong thing. Some people are just born to be happy being of service. I don't, again, see that as a negative. I can see that maybe, if you thought you were on the wrong side of that, and it was more of a pity party or a case of pity, instead of coming from a basis of love, then that might make it hard for you to swallow."

"That word you just used makes all the difference."

She looked up at him and asked, "What word?"

He hesitated, while she reviewed all she had just said.

"*Ah, … that* word." A smile twinkled across her features. "You mean the L-word." He nodded slowly. "Meaning that, because he was my brother, it was totally okay to do that because I did it out of love. But you're so unlovable that it couldn't possibly be the reason why I was interested in being with you, is that it?"

"Ouch," he said on a half laugh. "That's kind of blunt."

"And I would much rather be blunt and honest and discuss this," she stated, "than try to work my way through the mess that we can make up by ourselves in our own heads." She sighed, then shrugged. "I've got a lot to learn, and I know that this next six months will be challenging in many ways for me, particularly as the wedding approaches and as I grieve the loss of the relationship I thought I had with my brother—not because it's broken or because, in any way, I won't still be close to him but because how our relationship has changed. And it's taken me a while to realize that it's also okay to grieve for what was and yet to still look forward to what could be," she admitted. "Yet I wasn't quite prepared to let go of you at the same time."

Percy took a long slow deep breath. "And I would appreciate it if you don't let go of me," he said, with difficulty. "I *am* a project but a temporary one," he admitted. "I hadn't really realized it until just now, but I am somebody who'll need patience and time and adjustments. If you have the patience ..." He stopped, seemed to be waiting, while looking at her.

"I don't have a problem with that," she replied gently, "but I would really appreciate not being shut out anymore. Because that's the worst. Not knowing what you're thinking, not sure how to break an impasse that I didn't even know how it started. Communication is important to me."

"It's important to me too," he agreed, "and I didn't know how to get past that myself."

"Well, that's why life is all about practice," she noted. "If we got it perfect the first time, there would really be no reason for us to work on it, would there?"

"Does that mean I'm forgiven?" he asked hopefully.

"It means you're forgiven," she said softly, "as long as I hear some promise that we'll communicate better the next time we have an issue."

"Agreed." He looked at her. "And I'm really not a project for you, am I?"

"No, I wasn't thinking that at all," she stated. "But what you said also makes me rethink and realize that, from your perspective, you probably see yourself that way. And I hadn't considered that angle. So, from my perspective, if you're asking me to take you on, the answer's *absolutely*—with the understanding that this relationship is a project that we'll both have to work on and to talk about, as we walk through it."

"Now that's something I can agree with," he replied, smiling broadly.

She grinned, as she looked at him, noticeably happier now. "Half the people in the center are waiting to hear what happens to us after this talk. You know that, right?"

"I didn't know it entailed *half* of Hathaway House," he teased, "but I wouldn't be at all surprised. I got the impression that everybody here was thoroughly affected by what's going on."

"And healing is always the priority," she murmured. "I don't know what the consequences would be if we couldn't work this out," she said, with a frown. "And I'm really glad to hear that it won't be an issue today."

"No, not at all," he agreed, pointing to the basket. "I brought a picnic with me today, and I intended to enjoy it, but, at the same time, I was thinking that I shouldn't be alone because this was something we had planned on doing together."

"I think you'll find that that picnic basket is rather full because Dennis was really hoping that I would join you."

"Did he tell you where I was?"

"Not only did he, but so did Stan," she said, with an eye roll. "And I have to admit to being grateful to be here at the moment." Smiling, she stood, picked up the picnic basket, and sat it on the grass. "Oh, yeah, it's heavy."

"Do you have anywhere to be this afternoon?"

"More to the point," she asked, "do you?"

"Nope. I've got an extended break right now. I have to see the counselor afterward," he noted, with a wince.

"Sounds like good timing for it too," she muttered.

He laughed. "You know what? You could be right." He looked down and repeated, "I'm so sorry. … Am I forgiven?"

Because it wasn't the first time he'd asked, she got up and walked over, tilted his chin up and kissed him gently on the lips. "Yes. Completely."

He took a deep breath and asked, "What about that L-word you used?"

She flushed. "What about it?" she asked in a prevaricating manner.

"Remember how we are to be honest with each other?"

"Oh, totally," she agreed, yet groaned. "But how come I'm the one who has to go first?"

"You don't have to," he said instantly. "I'm not trying to put you on the spot. I just wanted you to know that that's how I feel."

"I'm not sure I understand. Are you saying you love me?" she asked hesitantly.

Astonished, he looked up at her and nodded. "Absolutely." He frowned. "I didn't make that clear, did I?"

She threw her arms around him, laughing.

He held her tight in his arms and whispered, "So let me make this very clear. Since the first moment I met you, I thought you were special. From the second moment I met you, I *knew* you were special. By the third time?" He tugged her closer. "I was smitten. By the fourth time"—he stared down at her gorgeous eyes—"you held my heart in your hands. And, when I thought that it wouldn't be the mutual relationship that I had hoped for, I was broken."

She reached up and stroked his cheek.

"And it really was hard to find a way to pull myself back together again, and now I'm very grateful for the fact that apparently I don't have to," he said, with a smile.

She knelt before him, holding his hands, and said quietly, "No, you don't have to because, just like you, it was a memorable meeting, and, just like you, that feeling grew and grew and grew. I was heartbroken when you shut me out and even more devastated when it seemed like we were broken before we had ever gotten anywhere."

"Oh, we got somewhere," he noted, "but one of the

things that I forgot about was to communicate."

She smiled. "Hiccups happen. We just don't have to stay broken."

"Agreed." He squeezed her hands and asked, "We're good?"

"We're good."

"Good. So where do you want to live when we leave this place? Of course that won't be anytime soon, but ..." She looked at him in surprise. He shrugged. "In my world, when we're good, we're *good*-good."

She leaned forward and asked, "How good?"

He leaned closer until their lips touched, and he whispered, "Marrying kind of good."

"Are you asking me to marry you?" she asked, her heart in her eyes.

He smiled. "Well, if I were to ..."

"No. No games," she said.

He nodded, grabbed her chin gently, and whispered, "Would you please do me the honor of becoming my wife at another time and at another place, when I can at least walk down the aisle without a wheelchair?"

"We can do it now. We can do it later," she whispered firmly against his lips. "As long as we do it before I'm old and gray."

At that, he burst out laughing, tugged her into his arms, so that she now sat on his lap, and he gave her the proper kiss he'd been wanting to give her since forever. When he finally lifted his head, he looked at her, smiled, and said, "I think I'll really enjoy the next few months."

She wrapped her arms around his neck and nodded. "Don't limit it to the next few months though. We've got a whole lifetime ahead of us. I'm looking forward to every minute."

Epilogue

QUINTON WALKED THROUGH the front door of the center, stopped, and looked around. When the receptionist looked up at her, Quinton replied, "I'm looking for Stan. And Shane."

"Stan's downstairs. Let me see where Shane is." The receptionist began clicking her keyboard. "He's booked up with rehab patients for the rest of the day. Unless you are one of his patients too?"

"I didn't have an appointment, but I thought I'd ask while I was here. So I'll just speak to Stan today."

The receptionist nodded. "He's downstairs."

"Downstairs?"

"Are you … Did you bring an animal for him?"

"No," she said. "I'm a lawyer."

"*Uh-oh.* Is he in trouble?"

The lawyer laughed. "Interesting response but, no, he's not in trouble. I am supposed to meet him here today. I am not exactly sure where to find him."

"He's literally downstairs. The vet clinic is on the ground floor," she explained. She gave Quinton further directions and said, "I'll let him know you're here."

"Thanks," she said. And smiling, she headed downstairs, looking for Stan. She'd met him a couple times at her office. But this time, with the paperwork, it was easier to just run by, and she was in the neighborhood. This way she could see what kind of operation he was really running and also get his signatures in person. As she walked through the double doors, she found another reception area. Waiting for the woman to get the message to Stan, Quinton wandered around and looked at the place. It was clean. It was efficient. People were standing outside. People were laughing, joking. No surprise there.

A dog was in the waiting room. Poor thing looked like she was terrorized just being here. But the owner was trying to reassure her and to cuddle her and to make her feel better. By the time the connecting door opened, and the woman and her dog were led to another room, Quinton wondered how long she would have to wait. She got up, walked to the receptionist again.

Just then Stan walked out through the connecting door and saw her. "Quinton, how are you?" he asked. "Come on in. I just got your message. I'm sorry if you've been waiting long."

She smiled and said, "It's all right. I wanted to see the place, what you were running here anyway. It's so much more than when I was here before."

"It's quite something now, isn't it?" he asked. "Wouldn't have been here without all the donors though. And Dani," he said, with an eye roll. "She's upstairs right now. Do you need to see her?" he asked, twisting to raise his eyebrows.

Quinton shook her head. "Nope, I don't think so, at least not this time."

"Good," he noted. "Pinning her down is almost as bad as pinning me down."

"I'll make note of that," Quinton teased. "This is beautiful here. You've done so much."

"Well, we've still got a ways to go," he added. "And you said you had paperwork for me?"

She nodded, realizing that he probably had a full schedule ahead of him. "Yep, I do." She dug in her briefcase and gave him a folder.

"Okay, I can go over these now. You didn't have to come by. You could have just sent them over."

"My brother's up there." She pointed upstairs. "And he's not too happy about it."

"Not too happy to be here or not too happy to be in this situation?"

"Not too happy to be in this situation," she confirmed. "Matter of fact, he's definitely not an easy person to be with."

"Interesting," he murmured. "Well, as you know, he'll get the best care here."

"I also wanted to talk to Shane, if I could get a moment with him, but the receptionist confirmed he's booked all day," she said. "As much as I've had some improvements, I've also had some setbacks, so I need Shane's help. I know he's here a lot."

"Full-time." Stan nodded. "I'm sure he'd want to talk to you. Particularly as you're an old—*previous*—patient."

"I am, indeed, *old* at least." She rolled her eyes.

He burst out laughing. "You don't look a day over thirty."

"Well, it's been many a day over thirty," she admitted, "and nothing like injuries to age you faster than you would like."

"True enough. And stress." He pointed at his head. "I'm not old myself, but, man, this white hair—which is a family trait—certainly doesn't help it."

"It's dignified looking," she said graciously.

He burst out laughing. "Well, that's one nice thing to call it." He grinned. "I knew I liked you."

At that, she smiled, then got back to business. "Paperwork?"

"Absolutely. Come on back to my office. Let's take care of business first." He led her to his office, where they both sat, while he read through the paperwork. Soon he nodded and signed the last page, initialing all the preceding pages. "Thank you, Quinton."

And, with that done, she stood. "Now you can get back to your patients."

"Ah, yes. I've got quite a roster coming up, but I've got a new vet coming along here pretty quickly," he noted. "And I'm looking forward to getting the help."

"Dani's fiancé, right?"

"That's correct," he said, with a smile. Stan escorted her to the elevator. "Let me know when you think you'll be in this area again, and I'll check with Shane about his schedule."

"I hate to even contact him," she noted. "I know how busy this place is."

"Let me talk to him and see when he's got an opening and I'll let you know."

"Thank you," she said in surprise. "Much appreciated." She looked around and smiled. "It really is a beautiful job you're doing here."

"It's a necessary one," he replied, "and when you're doing things for the right reasons …"

She nodded. "I agree with that wholeheartedly. Maybe I'll go see my brother while I'm here."

"What's his name?"

"Ryatt," she said. "He's only been here a couple weeks. But he's not making life easy for the others. I need to step in and maybe remind him that he doesn't have to be here if he doesn't want to and that he's taking a spot from somebody who could use it."

"Ouch, that would be some tough love," Stan noted, "because really this is the best place for him to be."

"I know it," she stated, "and I'm the one who convinced him to try to get in. Makes me sad to know he's wasting the opportunity he has here." She sighed and shook her head. "But, hey, that's not today's issue. I'll just stop in and say hey."

"I'll call you as soon as I talk to Shane," he promised. And, with that, he watched as she left.

She was a fine-looking woman. Even more, they'd clicked right from the beginning. He'd kind of hoped that maybe he could persuade her to go out with him once or twice. But to have her come here, where he worked, whether to visit her brother or to stay as a returning patient, that'd be perfect. She'd get the best help possible, while Stan had guaranteed time to see her.

He rubbed his hands together. Maybe things would turn in his direction for once.

This concludes Book 16 of Hathaway House: Percy.
Read about Quinton: Hathaway House, Book 17

Hathaway House: Quinton (Book #17)

Welcome to Hathaway House. Rehab Center. Safe Haven. Second chance at life and love.

Quinton had been a patient at Hathaway House in its first year. When she finally healed enough to move on with her life, she went into law and plowed forward. However, plowing forward may not have been the best answer for her physical injuries. While visiting Stan at the center, she collapses on her way to her brother's room, as he's a patient here now. The collapse shows a long-term issue, now an acute problem. After talking to Dani and Shane, Quinton's booked back into the center on a short-term basis.

Stan hurts for Quinton. She's an old friend, and he's watched her progress from his first year in business at Hathaway. He'd always had a crush on her but figured his window of opportunity had passed. Now with her once again as a patient, it feels like a second chance for a personal relationship, one he's more than willing to take.

Between her brother—who's not getting along at the center—and Quinton's own struggles to get back on her feet, thankfully she also has Stan and other old friends around, as Quinton takes the steps necessary to put her life back on track … in all ways.

Find Book 17 here!
To find out more visit Dale Mayer's website.
https://geni.us/DMQuintonUniversal

Author's Note

Thank you for reading Percy: Hathaway House, Book 16! If you enjoyed the book, please take a moment and leave a short review.

Dear reader,

I love to hear from readers, and you can contact me at my website: www.dalemayer.com or at my Facebook author page. To be informed of new releases and special offers, sign up for my newsletter or follow me on BookBub. And if you are interested in joining Dale Mayer's Reader Group, here is the Facebook sign up page.
http://geni.us/DaleMayerFBGroup

Cheers,
Dale Mayer

About the Author

Dale Mayer is a *USA Today* best-selling author, best known for her SEALs military romances, her Psychic Visions series, and her Lovely Lethal Garden cozy series. Her contemporary romances are raw and full of passion and emotion (Broken But ... Mending, Hathaway House series). Her thrillers will keep you guessing (Kate Morgan, By Death series), and her romantic comedies will keep you giggling (*It's a Dog's Life*, a stand-alone novella; and the Broken Protocols series, starring Charming Marvin, the cat).

Dale honors the stories that come to her—and some of them are crazy, break all the rules and cross multiple genres!

To go with her fiction, she also writes nonfiction in many different fields, with books available on résumé writing, companion gardening, and the US mortgage system. All her books are available in print and ebook format.

Connect with Dale Mayer Online

Dale's Website – www.dalemayer.com
Twitter – @DaleMayer
Facebook Page – geni.us/DaleMayerFBFanPage
Facebook Group – geni.us/DaleMayerFBGroup
BookBub – geni.us/DaleMayerBookbub
Instagram – geni.us/DaleMayerInstagram
Goodreads – geni.us/DaleMayerGoodreads
Newsletter – geni.us/DaleNews

Also by Dale Mayer

Published Adult Books:

Shadow Recon
Magnus, Book 1

Bullard's Battle
Ryland's Reach, Book 1
Cain's Cross, Book 2
Eton's Escape, Book 3
Garret's Gambit, Book 4
Kano's Keep, Book 5
Fallon's Flaw, Book 6
Quinn's Quest, Book 7
Bullard's Beauty, Book 8
Bullard's Best, Book 9
Bullard's Battle, Books 1–2
Bullard's Battle, Books 3–4
Bullard's Battle, Books 5–6
Bullard's Battle, Books 7–8

Terkel's Team
Damon's Deal, Book 1
Wade's War, Book 2
Gage's Goal, Book 3
Calum's Contact, Book 4

Kate Morgan

Simon Says… Hide, Book 1
Simon Says… Jump, Book 2
Simon Says… Ride, Book 3
Simon Says… Scream, Book 4
Simon Says… Run, Book 5

Hathaway House

Aaron, Book 1
Brock, Book 2
Cole, Book 3
Denton, Book 4
Elliot, Book 5
Finn, Book 6
Gregory, Book 7
Heath, Book 8
Iain, Book 9
Jaden, Book 10
Keith, Book 11
Lance, Book 12
Melissa, Book 13
Nash, Book 14
Owen, Book 15
Percy, Book 16
Quinton, Book 17
Hathaway House, Books 1–3
Hathaway House, Books 4–6
Hathaway House, Books 7–9

The K9 Files

Ethan, Book 1
Pierce, Book 2
Zane, Book 3

Blaze, Book 4
Lucas, Book 5
Parker, Book 6
Carter, Book 7
Weston, Book 8
Greyson, Book 9
Rowan, Book 10
Caleb, Book 11
Kurt, Book 12
Tucker, Book 13
Harley, Book 14
Kyron, Book 15
Jenner, Book 16
The K9 Files, Books 1–2
The K9 Files, Books 3–4
The K9 Files, Books 5–6
The K9 Files, Books 7–8
The K9 Files, Books 9–10
The K9 Files, Books 11–12

Lovely Lethal Gardens

Arsenic in the Azaleas, Book 1
Bones in the Begonias, Book 2
Corpse in the Carnations, Book 3
Daggers in the Dahlias, Book 4
Evidence in the Echinacea, Book 5
Footprints in the Ferns, Book 6
Gun in the Gardenias, Book 7
Handcuffs in the Heather, Book 8
Ice Pick in the Ivy, Book 9
Jewels in the Juniper, Book 10
Killer in the Kiwis, Book 11

Lifeless in the Lilies, Book 12
Murder in the Marigolds, Book 13
Nabbed in the Nasturtiums, Book 14
Offed in the Orchids, Book 15
Poison in the Pansies, Book 16
Quarry in the Quince, Book 17
Lovely Lethal Gardens, Books 1–2
Lovely Lethal Gardens, Books 3–4
Lovely Lethal Gardens, Books 5–6
Lovely Lethal Gardens, Books 7–8
Lovely Lethal Gardens, Books 9–10

Psychic Vision Series
Tuesday's Child
Hide 'n Go Seek
Maddy's Floor
Garden of Sorrow
Knock Knock...
Rare Find
Eyes to the Soul
Now You See Her
Shattered
Into the Abyss
Seeds of Malice
Eye of the Falcon
Itsy-Bitsy Spider
Unmasked
Deep Beneath
From the Ashes
Stroke of Death
Ice Maiden
Snap, Crackle...

What If…
Talking Bones
Psychic Visions Books 1–3
Psychic Visions Books 4–6
Psychic Visions Books 7–9

By Death Series
Touched by Death
Haunted by Death
Chilled by Death
By Death Books 1–3

Broken Protocols – Romantic Comedy Series
Cat's Meow
Cat's Pajamas
Cat's Cradle
Cat's Claus
Broken Protocols 1-4

Broken and… Mending
Skin
Scars
Scales (of Justice)
Broken but… Mending 1-3

Glory
Genesis
Tori
Celeste
Glory Trilogy

Biker Blues
Morgan: Biker Blues, Volume 1

Cash: Biker Blues, Volume 2

SEALs of Honor

Mason: SEALs of Honor, Book 1

Hawk: SEALs of Honor, Book 2

Dane: SEALs of Honor, Book 3

Swede: SEALs of Honor, Book 4

Shadow: SEALs of Honor, Book 5

Cooper: SEALs of Honor, Book 6

Markus: SEALs of Honor, Book 7

Evan: SEALs of Honor, Book 8

Mason's Wish: SEALs of Honor, Book 9

Chase: SEALs of Honor, Book 10

Brett: SEALs of Honor, Book 11

Devlin: SEALs of Honor, Book 12

Easton: SEALs of Honor, Book 13

Ryder: SEALs of Honor, Book 14

Macklin: SEALs of Honor, Book 15

Corey: SEALs of Honor, Book 16

Warrick: SEALs of Honor, Book 17

Tanner: SEALs of Honor, Book 18

Jackson: SEALs of Honor, Book 19

Kanen: SEALs of Honor, Book 20

Nelson: SEALs of Honor, Book 21

Taylor: SEALs of Honor, Book 22

Colton: SEALs of Honor, Book 23

Troy: SEALs of Honor, Book 24

Axel: SEALs of Honor, Book 25

Baylor: SEALs of Honor, Book 26

Hudson: SEALs of Honor, Book 27

Lachlan: SEALs of Honor, Book 28

Paxton: SEALs of Honor, Book 29

SEALs of Honor, Books 1–3
SEALs of Honor, Books 4–6
SEALs of Honor, Books 7–10
SEALs of Honor, Books 11–13
SEALs of Honor, Books 14–16
SEALs of Honor, Books 17–19
SEALs of Honor, Books 20–22
SEALs of Honor, Books 23–25

Heroes for Hire

Levi's Legend: Heroes for Hire, Book 1
Stone's Surrender: Heroes for Hire, Book 2
Merk's Mistake: Heroes for Hire, Book 3
Rhodes's Reward: Heroes for Hire, Book 4
Flynn's Firecracker: Heroes for Hire, Book 5
Logan's Light: Heroes for Hire, Book 6
Harrison's Heart: Heroes for Hire, Book 7
Saul's Sweetheart: Heroes for Hire, Book 8
Dakota's Delight: Heroes for Hire, Book 9
Tyson's Treasure: Heroes for Hire, Book 10
Jace's Jewel: Heroes for Hire, Book 11
Rory's Rose: Heroes for Hire, Book 12
Brandon's Bliss: Heroes for Hire, Book 13
Liam's Lily: Heroes for Hire, Book 14
North's Nikki: Heroes for Hire, Book 15
Anders's Angel: Heroes for Hire, Book 16
Reyes's Raina: Heroes for Hire, Book 17
Dezi's Diamond: Heroes for Hire, Book 18
Vince's Vixen: Heroes for Hire, Book 19
Ice's Icing: Heroes for Hire, Book 20
Johan's Joy: Heroes for Hire, Book 21
Galen's Gemma: Heroes for Hire, Book 22

Zack's Zest: Heroes for Hire, Book 23
Bonaparte's Belle: Heroes for Hire, Book 24
Noah's Nemesis: Heroes for Hire, Book 25
Tomas's Trials: Heroes for Hire, Book 26
Heroes for Hire, Books 1–3
Heroes for Hire, Books 4–6
Heroes for Hire, Books 7–9
Heroes for Hire, Books 10–12
Heroes for Hire, Books 13–15
Heroes for Hire, Books 16–18
Heroes for Hire, Books 19–21
Heroes for Hire, Books 22–24

SEALs of Steel
Badger: SEALs of Steel, Book 1
Erick: SEALs of Steel, Book 2
Cade: SEALs of Steel, Book 3
Talon: SEALs of Steel, Book 4
Laszlo: SEALs of Steel, Book 5
Geir: SEALs of Steel, Book 6
Jager: SEALs of Steel, Book 7
The Final Reveal: SEALs of Steel, Book 8
SEALs of Steel, Books 1–4
SEALs of Steel, Books 5–8
SEALs of Steel, Books 1–8

The Mavericks
Kerrick, Book 1
Griffin, Book 2
Jax, Book 3
Beau, Book 4
Asher, Book 5
Ryker, Book 6

Miles, Book 7
Nico, Book 8
Keane, Book 9
Lennox, Book 10
Gavin, Book 11
Shane, Book 12
Diesel, Book 13
Jerricho, Book 14
Killian, Book 15
Hatch, Book 16
Corbin, Book 17
The Mavericks, Books 1–2
The Mavericks, Books 3–4
The Mavericks, Books 5–6
The Mavericks, Books 7–8
The Mavericks, Books 9–10
The Mavericks, Books 11–12

Collections
Dare to Be You...
Dare to Love...
Dare to be Strong...
RomanceX3

Standalone Novellas
It's a Dog's Life
Riana's Revenge
Second Chances

Published Young Adult Books:

Family Blood Ties Series
Vampire in Denial

Vampire in Distress
Vampire in Design
Vampire in Deceit
Vampire in Defiance
Vampire in Conflict
Vampire in Chaos
Vampire in Crisis
Vampire in Control
Vampire in Charge
Family Blood Ties Set 1–3
Family Blood Ties Set 1–5
Family Blood Ties Set 4–6
Family Blood Ties Set 7–9
Sian's Solution, A Family Blood Ties Series Prequel
    Novelette

Design series
Dangerous Designs
Deadly Designs
Darkest Designs
Design Series Trilogy

Standalone
In Cassie's Corner
Gem Stone (a Gemma Stone Mystery)
Time Thieves

Published Non-Fiction Books:

Career Essentials
Career Essentials: The Résumé
Career Essentials: The Cover Letter
Career Essentials: The Interview
Career Essentials: 3 in 1

www.ingramcontent.com/pod-product-compliance
Lightning Source LLC
Chambersburg PA
CBHW070352200726
48294CB00003B/873